D1525539

WINTER ISLAND

James R. Nelson

James R. Nelson

Chapter 1

ERIC BALLARD SAT down in front of the desk of Michael Cohen and waited until he was off the phone.

"I'm sorry, Mr. Ballard. That was my wife. You know there's just some calls you have to take."

Eric smiled. "I understand."

A quick wave of panic passed over the accountant's face. "Oh, I'm sorry." His neck reddened slightly. "You're the author whose wife was killed. My wife's read some of your books. She...she was excited when she heard you had an appointment today." He stood and extended his hand. "Let me offer my condolences. What a terrible thing. I'm so sorry about your loss."

"Thank you."

"What has it been? A year? Have they found out who...did it?"

Eric shook his head. "It's been ten months. And no. Still no progress."

"I don't know what's happening to Chicago. I've lived here my whole life. Whoever would have thought ten years ago that the level of crime in this city would be where it's at today? It's getting out of control. All this time since your wife was killed and they haven't found out who did it. It's an abomination. Just an abomination. So, from what you told me over the phone, you're missing some money. What's going on?"

Eric sat back in his chair. "Once Claire died, I was going over her estate. As you know, both she and I are writers. We each have our own accounts for our book advances and royalties. She's been fortunate enough to have done very well with her

1

publisher. I don't know if you're aware, but her latest book was up for the coveted MacIntosh Award. That award is as lucrative as it is prestigious. Anyway, when I was reviewing the accounts, I could see withdrawals of five thousand dollars for the last eight months before she died. I've tried to figure out where this money went, but I've run into a complete roadblock. Nothing makes sense to me. I need someone who knows what they're doing to look into this."

"I've been a forensic accountant for over thirty years. I'm sure I can get to the bottom of this. Did you bring the copies that I requested?"

"Yes." Eric reached into an attaché case and pulled out a thick manila envelope. "Here's what I have. If you need something else, just let me know."

"Great. Give me a few days to look into this. I'll give you a call if I need anything more."

*****

Eleven hundred and forty miles to the south, heavy rain poured down on County Road 464 flooding the ditches to overflowing. Tropical storm Maybelle had stalled over central Florida for a day and a half and had dumped nine inches of rain onto the soggy landscape with no end in sight.

A sudden gust of wind snapped off a sand pine branch and sent it crashing into a faded billboard advertising a roadside attraction called *Doctor Merriweather's Menagerie of Human Oddities*.

Three miles away, Jake Kincaid looked up at the soggy canvas tent ceiling above his head. "If this damn rain doesn't stop soon, I think the whole mess tent's going to come crashing down on top of us." He looked around the table and slowly laid down his poker hand. "I got a full house. Three eight's and a pair of jacks."

Paul Sykes scratched his three-day old whiskers and let out a soft whistle. "Nice try, Jake my boy. I got me four tens." He smiled and reached for the pot.

Before he was able to scoop up any of the money, a huge man standing behind him grabbed him by the shoulders and lifted him three feet off his chair. "And you also got a few cards stashed under your ass. Coonie told me to keep an eye on you. The boys thought you were cheating them, but they never were able to catch you."

Jake whipped a switchblade from his pocket. "Drop him, Gaston. We'll take over from here. I don't care how good a carpenter he is, he's gonna pay for cheatin' the boys."

Gaston pulled the card cheat away. "No. I know what happened to the last cheat you guys caught. There'll be no more killin' while I'm here. I'll deposit him outside and give him half an hour to disappear. After that, he's all yours if you still want him."

Jake stared up at him. At over seven feet tall, Gaston was not someone he wanted to argue with. "Go ahead, then. Toss him out. But if me and the boys ever see his cheatin' face again—" He stuck the knife straight up in the top of the wooden table. "He'll never play another hand of poker."

Gaston walked to the front of the tent with Paul wiggling under his arm. Coonie pulled the canvas flap open as Gaston heaved Paul out into the wet night. There was a loud thud as he landed in a puddle of mud. "Best you get down the road as fast as you can," Gaston called out. "These boys don't play around."

Paul blinked a few times as the flap closed and the light from inside disappeared. He slowly moved. Nothing seemed to be broken. That had been one hell of a landing. He stood and looked around for his hat. It was impossible to see anything in the driving rain. To hell with it. He'd stolen that one, he could lift another one when the time came. He tried to wipe some of the cold mud off his shirt. It only made things worse. He looked up and down the road. Which way was it to the highway?

*****

Eric sat in front of his computer and stared at the screen. He'd been sitting there for two hours and only had three hundred and twelve words to show for it. He shut his laptop and walked out of the den.

He'd only started back writing a few weeks before, but it wasn't the same. His concentration was gone. Before Claire had died, he'd been able to knock out several scenes a day. He'd published a book a year for the last twelve years. Thankfully, they'd been well received by the public. But it was nothing compared to his wife's latest novel. *Death in a Small Town* had taken the publishing world by storm. When it was announced the book was in the running for the Macintosh Award, nobody thought she had much of a chance to actually win. How could she compete with William Simons or Joyce Carlson Smithers?

When she won, it had been bedlam. The calls, the baskets of flowers, the TV interviews. It was so exciting. Then the robbery happened. She was murdered two days before the Macintosh Award presentation. They were supposed to go to O'Hare the next morning to catch a flight to New York. Instead of accepting her award, Eric spent that day planning her funeral. He hadn't been able to write since.

He walked to the living room window and stared out over Lake Michigan. The view from the twenty-third floor was usually spectacular but tonight he couldn't see much. A thick fog bank had rolled in. A twenty-degree temperature change would do that.

He poured himself a whiskey on the rocks and settled into his favorite leather chair. When would he be able to write again? His outline was finished. What was stopping him? Maybe he needed to get away. Wasn't that what writer's retreats were for? A change of pace where a writer could get over their writer's block? Maybe a trip was in order.

Chapter 2

THE NARROW, TWO-lane blacktop highway merged seamlessly into the thick misty forest up ahead. Eric leaned closer to the windshield and blinked. It was the last few minutes before twilight turned to complete darkness. The time of day when your eyes played tricks on you. When everything was hard to see.

He jerked the steering wheel of his SUV just in time to miss a huge pothole. Either the spring thaw had been extremely hard on the road, or they weren't doing a very good job keeping Forest Highway 23 up to par. Eric lost count of the number of alignment wrecking catastrophes he'd dodged during the last twenty miles. He glanced down at the odometer. If his math was correct, he only had four more miles to go.

A brown blur exploded in his peripheral vision. He slammed on the brakes. A deer shot across the highway. Then another, and yet another. A doe and two fawns. Had he hit the last one? A quick tap maybe? He pulled over onto the shoulder and jumped out. Hit a fawn? That wouldn't be a good omen. He stepped in front of the car and stared at the bumper. There was no blood or hair.

Returning to the open driver's side door after a quick sigh of relief, he glanced up at the sky. When was the last time he had seen that many stars? Probably the last time he'd visited Red Cedar Cove ten months earlier for his wife's funeral. There weren't many stars visible from his condo. The place he was escaping from.

This visit would be different. He'd be by himself. No Claire. He settled back in the seat and put the vehicle in gear. Maybe this hadn't been such a good idea. Suddenly the logic of it didn't make much sense. He needed to get away from his wife's memories, but now he was going to be spending a few weeks in the house where she grew up. He shook his head. Now it sounded crazy, but back in Chicago it seemed like a good idea.

As he crested a hill, the amber glow of Red Cedar Cove's few streetlights greeted him from the bottom of a steep incline. The tiny community was bordered on three sides by state forest with an endless expanse of Lake Michigan to the east. He slowed at a blinking yellow light and turned left. Four blocks later he pulled into a driveway and parked in front of a large Victorian house.

Eric turned off the engine and remained seated. Maybe he should just turn around and go back home. How was this going to help with his grief? Being surrounded by Claire's past may make everything worse. What about her brother? He seemed amenable to the idea a week ago, but what if he was just being polite. Could he really say no to a grieving widower?

Eric took a deep breath and pushed open the car door. Clair's brother was coming down the porch steps. There was no turning back now.

"Welcome, Eric. How was the drive?"

Eric pulled his suitcase from the back seat. "Long and uneventful. Well not quite. I almost hit a deer a few miles up the road."

Harold Gustafson laughed. "I've hit my share. Nothing much you can do. They just come out of nowhere a hundred miles an hour. Come in. Let's have a drink."

After putting his suitcase in his wife's childhood bedroom, Eric returned downstairs.

Harold handed him a whisky on ice and pointed to a chair.

Eric sat and took a sip. "Ah, you remembered."

"We've shared many a drink in front of the fireplace," Harold replied. "I just wish Claire could be with us now to enjoy this." He paused. "How are you doing?"

Eric thought for a moment. "I guess I've been moving through all the stages of grief they tell you about. I think I'm probably at the mad part now. Thank you for having me. I had to get out of the condo. I'd go into our office and see the awards Claire won from her last book. How she had finally made it. Her new publishing contract." He blinked a few times. "And how it was all just taken from her." He paused and then snapped his fingers. "Just like that. In an instant. At…at the height of her success."

Harold took a sip from his drink. "I can't believe they haven't made an arrest."

Eric nodded. "I know. They tell me only about eighteen percent of all robberies in Chicago are solved."

Harold straightened in his chair. "Robberies? Claire was murdered."

Eric set his drink down. "She was, but the police think it was an unfortunate circumstance of the robbery. She walked in on them. The house was trashed."

"How could that happen? I've been to your place. It's beautiful. It's right in the heart of the loop on West Grand. There was a doorman, if I remember correctly."

"There was. Unfortunately, he got sick and called out. We went a few days without him." Eric looked around. "Where's Lillian? She still works here, doesn't she?"

Harold frowned. "It's so sad. Lillian? Are you kidding? Yes, she still works here. It will be thirty-six years in November." He got up and reached for Eric's empty glass. "Let's have another." He walked to an antique bar and refreshed their drinks.

8

"Did you know they optioned Claire's novel for a movie?" Eric asked.

Harold handed him a glass and sat back down. "Really?"

"I got the news two weeks ago." He glanced toward the stairs. "Is Lillian upstairs?"

"She's in her room. We're not the only ones mourning Claire's death. Lillian's taking it hard. She just about raised Claire, you know."

"Yes. They were very close. Claire used to talk to her at least once a week, even toward the end."

"She's been wearing black since the funeral. I told her it was okay to go back to her regular clothes, but she said it was some kind of Scandinavian tradition to wear black for a year."

Eric stood and walked to the window. "She's got two more months to go."

"Yes. Anyway, when she heard you were coming, I think it set her back a bit."

Eric looked surprised.

"Don't get me wrong. She's glad you decided to visit, but we've never seen you here without Claire."

Eric set his glass down. "Harold, maybe this visit wasn't such a good idea."

"Don't be ridiculous. Anyway, Lillian's prepared a wonderful meal. I just have to heat it up. I told her to take the evening off. Your room's all prepared. I hope you don't mind."

"Mind? No, that's fine. But maybe it would be better if I found another place to stay. It wasn't my intention to cause any additional heartache. God knows we've all had enough."

Harold waved his hand. "You haven't. This has been a terrible shock for everyone. We're glad to see you. Let's take our drinks into the library. I want to show you a manuscript I've been working on."

Eric followed his brother-in-law into a well-appointed library. Hundreds of books lined the walls. Worn leather chairs were next to two long oak tables. He inhaled. "God, I love the smell of old books."

"Watch this," Harold said, as he flipped a light switch. Several wall mounted light fixtures illuminated the library in soft flickering light.

Eric stared at the fixtures. "What are they?"

"I found these special bulbs. They look just like flickering flames. I thought it was the perfect look for this room." He pointed to the tables. "There are much brighter lights to read by. You know me, if it wasn't for these long Michigan winters, I'd probably be just fine with taking the electricity out of here entirely."

Eric smiled. "Yeah, sure. How about the refrigerator and the ice machine at the bar?"

"Oh. I never thought about that. I guess I'll have to settle for these new flame bulbs." Harold glanced at a stack of papers on one of the tables. "Before I bore you to tears about my new manuscript, how's your book coming?"

Eric rubbed his temples. "That's one of the reasons I wanted to come here. I haven't been able to write anything. I thought…" He paused. "I don't really know what I was thinking. I guess I was hoping a change of place would get me going again."

Harold's eyes swept the floor to ceiling bookshelves. "I've always found this room conducive to productivity. You're more than welcome to set your computer up here and have a go at it."

Eric turned away and wiped a tear from his eye. "Thank you. You don't know what that means to me."

Harold got up from his chair. "You need to be writing again. I'm going to heat up our dinner. Can I refresh your drink before I leave?"

Eric shook his head. "No. I'm a little tired from that long drive. If you don't mind, I'd like to take a quick nap before we eat. Do I have enough time?"

"Certainly. I'll work on my manuscript for half an hour, get things warmed up, and come and get you."

"Oh, how thoughtless of me. Your manuscript. You were about to tell me about it."

Harold pointed to the door. "Go get some sleep. We'll come back here after dinner, and I'll regale you with my brilliance then."

Eric walked up the staircase and entered Claire's room. He stood in the doorway for a minute, shocked at the room's sparse appearance. Most of her things had been removed. When they stayed on previous visits, the room had been cluttered with many of her mementos. During the second day of their visits, Eric would usually have to spend an hour straightening up. Claire had a tendency to lay her clothes everywhere. He wouldn't have to worry about that this trip. He sat on the edge of the bed. If only he could look forward to picking up her things once again.

Two hours later he joined Harold in the dining room for dinner. "How was your rest?" Harold asked.

"Very nice. But it felt strange to be in Claire's room without her."

"It was hard to get rid of her things. The posters and high school nick-knacks, but after a few months, I needed to face the reality that she was gone."

Lillian set down three plates of roast beef, mashed potatoes, and green beans. She took a seat next to Harold. They ate in silence for most of the meal.

Feeling slightly uncomfortable, Eric said, "Lillian, this is wonderful. From a man who's been eating his own cooking for almost a year, I can't tell you how good this tastes."

She smiled. "Thank you."

Harold reached for his coffee cup. "I hope you'll be able to do some writing while you're here."

"Me too. It's nice to get out of that apartment. I brought my outline. I'm thinking a new environment will help me collect my thoughts."

After they finished eating, they retreated to the library. Harold took a seat at the desk while Eric settled into a comfortable chair. "Okay. Tell me about your manuscript. I doubt if I'll be able to understand everything you're about to tell me about the Renaissance, but you did mention at dinner that your paper takes the view that the Renaissance was more an extension of the Middle Ages than a springboard from the past. Am I right?"

Harold nodded. "Yes. Let me explain."

It didn't take long for Eric to become completely lost in Harold's dissertation, but he nodded and added a thought whenever he could. It was apparent that both his late wife and her brother had benefitted greatly from their Ivy League educations. That wasn't surprising, since both of their parents had been college professors.

Eric, on the other hand, had attended a two-year community college and then graduated from Western Michigan University three hundred miles to the south. He smiled. That's why he was toiling away at a mystery novel, while Harold was crafting a scholarly tome on the historical significance of the Renaissance.

After two snifters of cognac, Eric started to relax. He felt comfortable in the rich surroundings of Harold's library. Unlike Claire, who frequently complained about how stifled she felt in the big Victorian house she had grown up in, her brother explained how happy he was to move in after their parents had passed away. The timing had been perfect. Harold's tenure at

Amherst had just finished, and he was ready to return to his roots - the Midwest.

Eric glanced around at the book covered walls. "Why do you think Claire was so anxious to leave?"

"She couldn't wait to get out of here," Harold said, staring into his glass of cognac. "She was excited about going to Wellesley, and I can see why. There's nothing here for young people. No jobs, not much of a social life. But I always enjoyed coming back home. Claire didn't. Once she left, she never looked back."

Eric took a sip from his drink. Harold was right. No, she didn't. In fact, she hated it when she had to return home for the requisite birthdays and other family celebrations. Thinking it would be best to change the subject, he asked, "Is that old diner still down the street?"

"Lucy's? Yes, it's still there. Why do you ask?"

"If it's all right with you, I'd like to get up early and walk over there for breakfast. I miss the crisp country air. We never get that in Chicago. Would you like to do that?"

Harold laughed. "Unfortunately, as time goes by, I seem to get up later and later. You go ahead. I'll stay back here and enjoy Lillian's scrambled eggs and bacon."

Chapter 3

TWENTY MINUTES AFTER seven the next morning, Eric stepped outside. He was glad he had put on a long-sleeved shirt. There was a chill in the air. A thin cloud of mist floated just above the waters of Lake Michigan.

The sidewalk next to the house was steep on its descent to the lake. He maneuvered it carefully. The water in the small harbor was crystal clear. Colorful rocks and pebbles along the bottom had a brilliance to them as the morning sunlight enhanced their luster. Every now and then a fallen log created a perfect hiding place for minnows and small fish that darted into its shadowy crevices as he walked by. He inhaled. The air was fresh, and the morning was quiet. No diesel fumes, honking car horns, or sirens. He had grown up in the country. Rural Wisconsin. It was good to be out of Chicago.

Up ahead was the neon sign for Lucy's Diner. Eric smiled. The rounded brushed aluminum building was unchanged from the fifties, as was the burned-out letter 'n' in the diner sign. He found it reassuring that some things never seemed to change.

As he pushed the door open, a pretty waitress almost collided into him. She was balancing a tray filled with three plates of pancakes and several white porcelain coffee cups. She quickly side-stepped him and called out, "Sit wherever you want, darling."

Eric slid into a shiny red vinyl booth. Darling? She probably used that term for everyone. He glanced around. The restaurant was smaller than he remembered. Claire had insisted they eat here at least once during every visit. It was strange. Why did she like it so much? Certainly not for the food. She never frequented diners in Chicago. Probably an excuse to get out of the family home for an hour or two. Who knew? Claire was a strange combination of eccentricities. Private college, but down to earth…when she wanted to be. He drummed his fingers against the Formica table. Claire wasn't a combination of anything now. Only memories.

Enough of that. He looked around. Only a few of the booths were occupied. He reached for a menu. The young waitress reappeared holding an order pad. "What you got a taste for, handsome?"

"I could really use a cup of black coffee. Then, how about the Lucy special?"

"How you want your eggs?"

"Over easy."

She scribbled his order down, gave him a quick smile, and headed toward the kitchen.

The front door opened. A man stepped in holding a newspaper under his arm. Immediately, Eric remembered he knew him. How could he not. It was Denton Morris, the only black man in Red Cedar Cove. At least that's what Claire had told him, and with a population of about two hundred and fifty residents, it was probably true. Denton had been over at the house for her brother's birthday celebration the year before. Claire said he used to be a writer.

Denton surveyed the room, apparently looking for an empty booth when he spotted Eric. He hesitated for a moment, then walked over and extended his hand. "I'm very sorry for your loss, Mr. Ballard."

Eric motioned for him to sit down. "Thank you. Please, call me Eric."

Denton Morris slid into the seat opposite him. "I was shocked. Just shocked when I heard about what happened to your wife."

Eric nodded. "Yes. It's been a blow for everyone."

"Did you know we were going to have a celebration here in town for her?"

"A celebration?"

"Yes. When she won the Macintosh Book Award. It was Lyle's idea."

Eric searched his memory. "Lyle?"

"Lyle Lapeer. Our librarian."

Eric's eyebrows arched. "Really? He was going to have a party because Claire won the Macintosh Award?"

"He did have it. But after what happened, it was more a memorial than a celebration."

The young waitress reappeared and set Eric's breakfast on the table. She pushed an extra coffee toward Denton. "What are you having, Mister D? Your usual?"

"Yes, Cheryl."

She stepped back. "Did you read my short story yet?"

Denton shook his head. "No, not yet. It'll be done by Monday. I promise."

She shrugged. "Okay. I'm going crazy waiting to hear what you think."

As she walked away, Eric said, "Does everybody in the whole town write? I'm staying at Claire's brother's place, and he's working on a manuscript. You must write, or you wouldn't be reading that young lady's story. It's apparent that she writes. Has Red Cedar Cove turned into some kind of writers' colony, and I haven't heard about it?"

Denton laughed. "Not quite. I used to write a long time ago. Cheryl found out about it somehow, and now she's talked me into critiquing some of her work." He watched her step into the kitchen. "Actually, I'm quite enjoying it. She's not bad. Has a tendency to head hop and sometimes she gets mixed up with her tenses, but her stories move along, and they're interesting."

"Tell me more about this celebration."

Denton blew on his coffee. "Lyle was all excited about a hometown person winning the Macintosh Prize, so he said he was going to have a party over at the library on the night your wife was supposed to accept her award." Denton glanced down at the table. "But of course, that didn't happen. It turned out to be just a small gathering."

Eric had a vision of Claire lying on the floor of their study covered in blood. He needed to change the subject. "Lyle Lapeer? He must be from this area's famous Lapeer family."

Denton nodded. "He certainly is. He's the last one left. He never married, as far as I know. Kind of sad. The impact that family had on Red Cedar Cove, and all."

"Isn't the library named after his family?"

"Lyle tells everyone his grandfather put up the money for it, but I think the money really came from Dale Carnegie, like so many of those small-town libraries did. Not that Lyle's grandfather couldn't have afforded it. He's the guy who started Lapeer Forestry Products. At one time they owned all the land around here."

The waitress returned and set down a plate with two pancakes and a side of bacon. "Here you go, Denton. Enjoy."

"Thank you, Cheryl." He looked back at Eric. "There was no town here then. They needed a port to ship out the lumber, so that's how Red Cedar Cove got started." He picked up a piece of bacon. "The town had over five hundred people living in it at one time."

They ate in silence for a few minutes, and then the conversation turned to the end of fall and football teams. When the waitress refilled their coffee cups, Eric asked, "Are you from here, Denton?"

"No. I was born and raised in Detroit. My father moved us up here when I was in junior high. He could see I was headed in the wrong direction. I'm glad he did. I like it here. The people are friendly, the place never seems to change. I think that's what I liked about it most of all. In Detroit, things were always changing. You'd drive down a street that you were familiar with, then six months later, you hardly knew the place. It isn't like that here." He looked around. "Case in point. This diner probably looks exactly like it did the day they opened sometime in the fifties." He smiled. "I'm not a man of the times. No cell phone. No computer. I still use a typewriter."

"Really?"

"Yes, sir. It's getting a little harder to find ribbons, but I've stocked up. Probably have enough to last me the rest of my life."

When Cheryl returned with their checks, Denton grabbed them. "I've got this."

Eric reached out. "No, I insist."

"Next time." Denton stood. "It was nice seeing you again. I'm going to miss those wonderful conversations I used to have with your wife. She always kept me up to date on what was happening in the ever-changing publishing world."

"Well, thank you for breakfast."

As Denton exited the restaurant, Eric thought about Lyle Lapeer wanting to have a party in Claire's honor. How would she have taken that? She didn't like coming back to the area. Maybe she would have thought it was nice. No telling.

He finished his coffee, pulled a few singles from his wallet for a tip, and stepped outside. The air was still crisp and cool. The mist had burned off the lake. Feeling full from breakfast, Eric decided to walk the few blocks over to the library.

He turned right on Lake Shore Road. Most of the streets along that part of town were named for trees that were found in the area, maple, elm, birch, and so on.

Once he crossed the two-lane blacktopped road that led into town, the street signs changed. They were named for fish that were found in the Great Lakes. The surroundings now took on a decidedly different look. It was obvious the rich people lived along the tree named streets.

The library had been constructed on top of a small hill off Whitefish Road. The domed, red-brick, and sandstone building was one of the few places in Red Cedar Cove Claire seemed to enjoy, besides the diner.

Eric stepped between two massive columns and was about to pull the door open when his cell phone went off. He glanced at the screen. It was Michael Cohen, the accountant. "Hello. I'm fine, thank you. No, you're not bothering me. Have you been able to find out anything?" He listened. "An offshore bank in the Bahamas? No. I have no idea why money would be going there. But now I'm worried. Won't that be almost impossible to trace?"

Eric listened as Michael explained recent legislation had made it somewhat easier to investigate those types of accounts. He said he was still working on it, but he couldn't guarantee he'd be able to trace where the money was really going. He was just calling to give Eric a quick update and let him know he was still investigating.

"Thank you for the phone call. I'm looking forward to hearing from you again." He shoved his phone back in his pocket. An offshore bank? What was that all about? Was Claire diverting funds from her own account?

Eric pulled the door open. Once again, the familiar aroma of books hit him. The rich leather smell of Harold's library was replaced by a mustier scent many older book depositories seemed to have in common, no matter where they were located.

A small man in his early sixties sat hunched over the desk. Was that Mr. Lapeer? Eric stared at him for a moment. Had they ever met? The librarian didn't look familiar. Should he introduce himself?

Eric decided against it. He walked past the main desk and disappeared between a narrow stack of books. Maybe he could find Claire's novel somewhere. After a few minutes of searching, there it was. Three copies of *Death in a Small Town*. They were in the mystery section under BAL. He looked for his novels. They weren't there.

Chapter 4

ROY SUNDSTROM SET down his paint brush and wiped his forehead. How long could he continue with these endless repairs? The twelve cabins perched along the lakefront were over sixty years old. Built in the mid-fifties, not many tourists enjoyed their quaint charm anymore. Everyone now days was looking for luxury. How many times had he been asked if the cabins came equipped with hair dryers? Hair dryers. What a joke. It was all he could do to keep the septic tank working. Two more years. He needed to stay open at least two more years. With lakefront property increasing in value, the next owners could buy the place, tear down the buildings, and put up whatever the hell they wanted. He'd be roasting his ass off in Bullhead City, Arizona like his friend Ivan.

He watched as the beat-up car that belonged to Christine Nash, from cabin number three, drove by. He returned her wave. Nice lady. Pretty, too. It was a shame what happened to her. He hoped she and her son would be able to work their way out of a bad situation.

He'd been surprised when she accepted his invitation to go out to dinner. Maybe she felt obligated since he'd given her a deal on the rent. It didn't matter. He enjoyed her company. He was lonely. Had it really been seventeen years ago that his wife had left him? Yes. Seventeen long, lonely years. It hadn't come as a big surprise. Everyone told him what to expect. It was hard to keep a marriage together after something like that. Just like the cabins, their relationship slowly deteriorated after his daughter disappeared.

Roy pulled over a metal chair, sat down, and took out a smoke. One more window frame to go. He lit a cigarette and inhaled deeply. Barbara. Where was she? Had she run away like his wife kept hoping or had one of the help done something to her? She had her share of boys coming around. She was beautiful like his wife.

Roy took a drag from his cigarette, stood, and squinted at the remaining window frame. Maybe he'd ask Christine out again. Why not? What did he have to lose?

*****

A huge dog bounded to the edge of the sandy Lake Michigan shoreline. "Hold on, King. We have to wait for Darrell." The black German shepherd stopped and turned toward his owner. Twelve-year-old Buddy Nash glanced at his watch and surveyed the shoreline. Where was Darrell? It was getting late. He only had an hour and a half to get over to the island and back. There were a lot of things that had to be done.

He waited for another ten minutes and then snuck over to his neighbor's yard. Buddy slid an old dented aluminum canoe out from under the dilapidated porch of the cabin next door. He grabbed a paddle, tossed in a hammer he had hidden in the tall weeds, and pushed the boat to the shoreline. "Okay, King. Get in."

The big dog jumped into the canoe and lay down behind the empty front seat. Buddy pulled off his socks and sneakers, tossed them into the boat, and then rolled up his jeans. He gave the canoe a big shove and hopped in.

The water was calm. It only took ten minutes to paddle over to Winter Island. King jumped out as soon as the canoe sunk into the soft, white Lake Michigan sand. Buddy followed, pulled the boat onto the shore, picked up the hammer, and ran down a narrow trail to the middle of the Island.

A pile of two-by-fours and plywood lay scattered under a huge oak tree. The wood had been scavenged from several abandoned boats that had run aground many years before. Buddy gazed up into the branches of the tall tree. Eight three-foot boards had been fastened up the tree to a small platform.

He looked down at several pieces of plywood that had been nailed together. This was going to be the first wall of the tree house. How was he going to get it up there without Darrell's help?

Buddy walked over and gripped the wall by its edge. He struggled to lift it. It was too heavy. He let go and jumped back as it dropped to the ground with a thud. That damn Darrell. There was no way he'd be able to do it by himself. He stared down at a pile of twisted nails. He and his friend had spent several hours rummaging through old lumber for them. Buddy knelt down next to a flat stone. He didn't need Darrell to straighten them out.

He spent the next forty-five minutes tediously turning twisted nails into straight ones. He managed to only hit his fingers three times. The last blow caused a very noticeable blood-blister. How was he going to explain that to his mother? If she found out he'd snuck the canoe out and paddled over to the island, he'd probably be grounded until Christmas.

He tossed the hammer down. Damn nails. King stood up and sniffed the air. Buddy turned. "What is it? What're you smelling?"

The dog let out a deep bark and bounded down a narrow trail through the woods. Buddy jumped up and chased after him. After following King for several minutes, the dense tree canopy cleared. King was standing on his hind legs intently staring at a fat raccoon he had treed.

Buddy leaned against the tree and tried to catch his breath. "Leave it alone, King. You don't want to pick a fight with him." As he tried to pull the dog away, something in the distance caught his eye. Buddy walked toward the clearing. A thick tangle of vines almost completely surrounded a small, rundown shack at the edge of the water. He stopped. A rusted tin roof poked out from the overgrowth. A door hung at an angle from only one hinge. The window next to it was broken.

Buddy eased up to the structure. Maybe this could be their clubhouse? It would be a lot easier to fix up than trying to get three more walls put together and hoisted up into that big tree. He stopped at the entrance and poked his head in. A small potbelly stove sat in one corner next to a table with two wooden chairs. A third chair was on its side.

A scurrying sound came from across the room. Buddy spun around. A narrow discolored mattress sat on top of a rusted bedframe. Something moved. A pair of beady eyes stared out from a dark hole in the mattress. Was it a mouse? No. Too big for a mouse. Buddy took a step back. A huge rat exploded from the stuffing. It was followed by two more.

Buddy jumped outside and tried to slam the door. He ran back to where King was staring up at the raccoon. The wind had picked up. Buddy looked at his watch. It was time to leave. It was going to take longer to paddle back to the mainland; and his mother would be home soon. "Come on, King. It's time to go."

*****

Lillian Olsen was vacuuming when Eric entered the foyer of the Gustafson house. She shut off the machine and gave him a quick hug. "How are you doing?"

Eric was taken aback. First at the stiff embrace, then by the dark apparel that covered her from head to toe. He remembered what Harold had told him about her mourning attire. He had been surprised to see it. "Thank you, Lillian. I'm doing okay, I guess. But I could ask the same of you. I know how close Claire was to you."

As Lillian tried to smile, tears formed in the corners of her eyes. She nodded. "Harold's in the library. He told me to have you join him when you returned."

Eric walked down the long hallway. Was there some way he could convince Lillian that it would be fine to start wearing her normal clothes? Her appearance only made things worse. He wanted to get away from his grief. To start writing again. Not to be plunged back into memories of Claire's funeral.

Harold looked up from his manuscript as Eric entered the library. "How was the diner?"

"It was nice. Typical diner breakfast. Large portions, very reasonable, and the coffee was great. Denton Morris sat with me. It was nice seeing him again." He paused. "Did you know there was supposed to be a celebration in town the night Claire was going to receive the Macintosh Award?"

"I did. I was a little surprised, considering what was in my sister's book."

Eric stopped. "You were? Why was that?"

Harold motioned for him to take a seat. "Well, Claire's book was quite dark. A child being murdered and all. There were more than a few references to things in Red Cedar Cove. Because of that, I found it a little strange that the townspeople would be so eager to celebrate it."

Eric pulled over a chair and sat down. "Are you kidding? I edited her first draft and all of her rewrites. I never picked up on anything related to Red Cedar Cove."

Harold grinned. "Probably just my overactive imagination. Claire always told me I should have been the one in the family to write fiction. Anyway, you mentioned you had breakfast with Denton. How is he? I always liked that guy. Did you know he was quite famous in the early sixties?"

"No. Famous for what?"

"He wrote a series of books that were geared toward young boys. Kind of like the Hardy Boys, but his books leaned more toward kids that lived in urban areas."

"I wish I would have known that. I would've liked to have heard more about them."

Harold thought for a moment. "Maybe it was best you didn't."

Puzzled, Eric asked, "Why?"

Harold closed his manuscript and pushed himself away from the table. "Well like I said, that was back before equal rights had taken off. From what I heard, his books were doing very well until either his publisher, or readers, found out he was black. Once that got out, his sales dried up, and he was dropped."

Eric stared at him. "Are you kidding? That's terrible. You're right. I'm glad I didn't walk into that topic. What a shame. He's such a nice guy. He's reading some stories our waitress has been giving him. She's young. I bet she has no idea of what happened to him."

"I'm sure she doesn't."

Eric shook his head. "On a cheerier note, do you know of any hiking trails around here? I'd love to find a trail or two to take some time in the next few days. I enjoyed my walk so much this morning."

"I certainly do." Harold grinned. "Not that I know about them firsthand or anything. There's some trails up at Ledge Park. Supposed to be real pretty. A great view overlooking the town and the lake." He walked over to one of the floor-to-ceiling bookcases and pulled out a thin paperback. "This book may be a little dated, but it has all the trails around the area. I doubt much has changed since it was published." He handed it to Eric.

"Thank you." Eric glanced at the cover.

Harold snapped his fingers. "I know!"

Eric looked up. "What?"

"Tomorrow I'm having lunch with my friend, Brian. He lives near the park. Why don't you come with me? I'll show you where the trails start."

Eric shook his head. "No. I don't want to do that."

Harold looked surprised. "Why not? You know Brian. He's always hanging around here."

"Why not? Two reasons. First, I wasn't invited. Secondly, remember how bent out of shape he was when I started dating Claire?"

"Eric, that Claire business is ancient history. A childhood crush. You weren't invited because he didn't know you'd be here when he asked me to come over." He stepped over to the telephone. "I'll call him. He'd be delighted to see you again."

"Wait! No, please—"

Harold ignored him and dialed his friend's number.

Chapter 5

BUDDY NASH SAT on a broken rocking chair under the open porch of cabin number three and watched as the rain poured down. His mother had told him it was going to rain all day. So far she'd been right. He glanced back down at the comic book he'd been reading. It wasn't keeping his interest. He'd read it a hundred times before. New ones were hard to come by.

An old car pulled up and slowed to a stop in front of the cabin next door. A man jumped out and ran for the porch. He was holding a newspaper over his head with one hand and clutched a small suitcase in the other. He fumbled with the key, pushed the door open, and disappeared inside.

Buddy stood up and looked over at the car. Was anyone else coming? Any kids? He sat back down. The man seemed to be by himself. Too bad. A few weeks ago, there had been a family from Indiana with three kids staying there. That had been fun. Those boys sure knew how to swear. They owned a lot of comic books too. His mother had been happy when they moved on.

A few minutes later the man exited the cabin and sat down on a chair under a small overhang. He lit a cigarette and took a drink from a pint bottle of whiskey. Buddy snuck a look. His hair was cut short and he was wearing a white tee-shirt. His biceps were big. Bigger than any Buddy had ever seen before. Even bigger than his dad's.

The man looked over. "What you reading?"

Startled, Buddy closed his book. "Nothing much. Just an old Batman comic."

The man took a long swig from his bottle. "Batman, eh? Those used to be my favorites when I was a kid. Hey, I noticed there's a pile of comic books in here. You want them?"

Buddy's eyes got wide. "There is?"

"Yeah. I don't think they clean these places too good. I'll get them." He disappeared back into the cabin. When he returned, he was holding a stack of books. "They're yours if you want them."

Buddy tried to dodge the raindrops as he ran over to the man's porch. "Wow. These were the ones from the family that stayed here before you. I can't believe they just left 'em."

"Here you go." He pointed to a chair next to his. "You got a minute? Sit down."

Buddy crawled into the chair and counted the comics. "There's twelve here. Thanks, mister."

"The name's Jack. Jack McGill. What's yours?"

"Buddy Nash."

"How long you staying, Buddy? You on your way someplace?"

Buddy felt his cheeks flush. "Ah, no. We...we're living here for a while."

"Nothing wrong with that. This place seems okay. They got a hell of a view of the water. I'll be staying here for a while myself."

Buddy looked over at him. "Really? Ma say's we gotta leave by Halloween. They close the cabins up then. Close them up for the winter."

Jack nodded. "Yep, that's what the man told me. Where you going to go then?"

Buddy shook his head. "I don't know. Every time I ask Ma about it, she gets mad. Tells me to shut up."

"You got a dad?"

Buddy ran his fingers over the smooth finish of the top cover. "I did. He got killed in a car crash. Some drunk hit him when he was coming home from work. We used to live in a real apartment then. Over in Trout Creek. I even had my own room."

Jack lit another cigarette. "That's too bad about your old man. Your mother work?"

"Sometimes. What about you? You're not headed anywhere?"

Jack grinned. "I guess you could say that."

Buddy looked back down at his stack of comics. What did that mean?

His mother stepped out from the cabin. "Buddy, get over here."

He stood up. "Hey, I gotta go. Thanks for the books."

"No problem. Enjoy them. We'll talk later."

Buddy's mother ushered him inside. "What do you have there?"

"That guy gave me all these comic books. Those kids from Indiana left them in the cabin. Just left them. Can you believe it?"

She grabbed him by the shoulders. "What I can't believe is, I'm trying to take a nap, and I hear you sitting with some stranger talking your head off. What's wrong with you? Who is that guy? He could be some escaped convict or some serial killer. And you're just sitting next to him telling him all about our dirty laundry."

"I never said anything about laundry. He asked about Dad. He seems like a nice guy. He's going to be living there, like us."

"Buddy, what have I told you over and over? You have to be careful. Everyone out there isn't nice. There are some really bad people around. You need to be more careful."

Buddy held up the stack of comics. "But look. He gave me these."

His mother rolled her eyes. "The better to kidnap you with, you dummy. Look, I've got to go to Mrs. Franklin's house over on Maple Street. She's got some housekeeping for me to do. I want you to stay here while I'm gone."

"She wants you to work on a Sunday?"

"As little work as I've been able to find, I'm quite happy with working on Sunday." She glanced down at the stack of comic books. "It looks like you've got plenty to keep you busy. Stay away from that man. Do you understand?"

"Yeah. Like I said, he seems to be a nice guy."

"Maybe he is. But I need to meet him and hear what his story is before I want you talking to him again."

"How long are you going to be gone?"

"From what Mrs. Franklin said, maybe three hours. I'll be home for supper." She glanced out the window. "It looks like it may clear up. If it does, you can go outside. Remember, stay away from that man next door."

"Can I go over to Darrell's house?"

"Only if it stops raining. I'm taking the umbrella." She put on a coat, grabbed the umbrella, and hurried out the door.

Half an hour later, a streak of blue broke through the clouds over the lake. The rain stopped and the wind died down. Buddy stepped onto the porch and looked over at cabin number four. The old car was gone. Winter Island shimmered in the distance. The tree house!

Buddy ran back inside and dialed the phone. "Darrell, can you get over here? My mom's gone for a few hours. I thought we could head over to the island and get that wall up. You can? Good. See you in a few."

Ten minutes later, the boys dragged the canoe out from under the porch next door and launched it in the water. Buddy sat in the back and tried to peer around his huge German shepherd. He yelled at Darrell, "I can't believe you forgot to bring your paddle. It's gonna take us twice as long to get over there."

"I'm sorry. You sounded like you were in a big rush. I didn't have time to sneak it out of the basement."

Buddy dug his paddle into the water. Twenty minutes later, the canoe knifed into the soft white sand of the shoreline. They jumped out and headed to the middle of the island.

When they got to the tree house, Buddy pointed to a pile of nails. "Look. I straightened all of these out yesterday."

Darrell walked over to the plywood wall they had constructed. "Good. We'll need them to nail this up there real tight. We sure don't want it falling down." He picked up a length of rope and tied it around the structure. "I'll climb up to the base and pull. You stay down here and help it up from the bottom."

Buddy stared at the rope. It looked old. "What if it breaks?"

Darrell laughed. "Guess I'll have to bury you out here and paddle back all by myself." He climbed a few of the wooden steps. "Come on. Get ready to push."

After several false starts, they finally got the wall nailed in place. King barked and circled the base of the tree. Buddy looked out the small glassless window. "Shut up, King. You can't come up here." He turned to Darrell. "One wall down, three more to go. This is going to be so cool."

Darrell looked around. "Yeah. Too bad we don't have the other ones made yet."

Buddy grabbed him by his shoulders. "Hey! I got to show you something."

"What?"

"You'll see. I found it yesterday when King chased a big ol' raccoon." Buddy scrambled down the tree ladder and jumped onto the ground. He searched the woods. Where was that trail?

Darrell landed next to him. "What is it?"

Buddy pointed. "It's this way. Follow me." They made their way through the woods until they reached the clearing. "Look," Buddy said. "It's a shack."

"Wow. Look at that." Darrell turned. "Is it empty? Maybe we could —"

"I know what you're thinking. No, it's not empty. It's full of rats."

"Rats?"

"Yeah. I was thinking the same thing. Ready-made clubhouse. I went in and ran right back out. There's a mattress in there that was full of the damned things."

"Let's go see." Darrell took a step toward the shack.

"Okay but be careful. I knew a friend once who had a mouse run up his pant leg. Made the guy pee his pants."

Darrell laughed. "Come on. You're making that up." As he approached the run-down building, Buddy said, "Watch out. That door's about to fall off."

His friend slowly pulled it open and stepped inside. "Hey, it's got a stove and a table and chairs." He looked around. "I don't see any —"

A lump appeared in the middle of the mattress and moved toward the edge. Shrill squeaks filled the shack. Just like the day before, several rats fell to the floor.

As Darrell turned to run, he collided with Buddy. They both fell down near the stove. "Get off me!" Buddy yelled. He scrambled for the door. One of the rats ran outside. King barked and started after it.

Buddy tried to call him back, but he was laughing too hard. "Man, I thought for sure one of those monsters was going to run right up my pant leg."

"Me too. I couldn't get out of there fast enough." Darrell flung himself onto the ground. "You know what? I think this must be the place my dad told me about last year."

"What place?"

"The shack where a crazy old hermit used to live out here on the island all by himself."

Buddy glanced over at the dilapidated structure. "A hermit?"

"That's what my dad said. Lived here for a long time. Used to take a rowboat over to the mainland a few times a week. They didn't see him for a while. Someone came to check on him and found him dead in his bed."

"Oh, gross! I bet those rats killed him."

Darrell picked up a stick and threw it at Buddy. "I don't think his mattress was full of rats when he lived here, dummy."

Buddy thought for a moment. "Yeah, probably not. But you never know. Look at that place. I bet there were plenty of things crawling around inside when he lived there. Do you think the boat's still here"?

"I don't know. Let's find out."

Buddy followed his friend as he walked behind the cabin. Darrell pointed. "Look." An old rowboat was turned upside down about twenty feet from the shore.

"I guess you're right. This must be the hermit's shack." Buddy looked up at the sky. "Hey, we better head back. Look how dark it is over there."

"Oh, that looks bad. Let's go."

By the time they got back to the canoe, the wind had picked up, and the waves had gotten bigger. Darrell looked worried. "You need to have your dog lie down. We better stay on our knees, too. It's going to be kind of rough out there."

34

"I know. Damn it, Darrell. I sure wish you would've brought your paddle."

Darrell searched the beach for something to use. "Here. I'll try this piece of driftwood. It's not a paddle, but it's better than nothing."

They shoved the canoe into the water. Buddy said, "King, lie down." The dog flattened himself against the bottom.

Darrell stuck his board into the water and looked over at the mainland. "I don't know. It looks bad."

"What do you want to do? Spend the night? If your mom finds out we've been sneaking out here, she'll have a fit worse than my mom will."

Darrell moved his makeshift paddle through the water. "Let's go."

Luckily the wind was toward their backs which made the trip to shore go quicker than they thought. Almost an inch of water was in the canoe by the time they landed in front of the cabins. King jumped out and shook his coat.

They dumped the water out and shoved the boat back under the neighboring cabin. Buddy said, "The guy that's staying here found a bunch of comic books and gave them to me this morning."

Buddy went inside and returned with the stack of comics. He handed them to his friend. "There's Superman, Batman, and a bunch of other stuff."

Darrell leafed through them. He held one up. "You a fan of Little Lulu now?"

Buddy smiled. "That one's for you." They spent the next half hour looking through the pile. Gravel crunched in the driveway. Buddy looked up. "Mom's home."

His mother got out of the car and walked up to the porch. "Buddy, has that dog been in the lake again? He smells like dead fish."

Buddy looked over at his friend. "Ah, yeah. He ran after some ducks."

"Put those books down. Come in the house and get some soap. You and Darrell can wash King while I make supper."

"Okay, Ma. Come on, Darrell. You can rinse."

Chapter 6

PAUL SYKES SAT at a bar in Trout Creek and cradled a glass of whiskey. "Damn. What's with this weather? I can't warm up. Guess I spent too much time in Florida."

The bartender ignored Paul's comments and continued to wash glasses.

Slightly irritated, Paul called out, "Hey, you're not very damn friendly. Don't you remember me? I used to come in here all the time a few years back. You're Frankie, aren't you?"

The bartender dried a glass and set it on a shelf. He stepped in front of Paul and crossed his arms. His large biceps bulged against his tight black shirt. "Yeah, I'm Frankie, and I do remember you. I remember how you cost me about eight hundred dollars in broken furniture the second year I owned the place."

Paul downed his drink. "I think you got me mixed up with my buddy, Willard. If I remember correctly, I was the guy who pulled my friend off that ex-Marine." Paul pushed his empty glass over to Frankie. "Hit me up with another one, will you?"

The bartender poured him another shot. "That's not how I remember it, but I'm not going to argue with you."

Paul reached for the glass. "Speaking of Willard, how is the old goat?"

"The old goat's dead."

Paul's drink froze halfway to his lips. "Dead? You got to be kidding. What happened?"

"Your buddy had a heap of problems. He got arrested a few times for picking fights, petty theft, things like that. I guess he had enough. He built himself a shack over on Winter Island and lived there all by himself. About a year ago, last October I think, they hadn't seen him around town much. Somebody went to check on him and found him dead."

"Dead? From what? He was only in his late forties, wasn't he?"

The bartender scratched his head. "He looked older than that to me, but maybe it was that scraggly beard and long hair. Heart attack. That's what the word was. I don't know, maybe he killed himself. Like I said, he had a lot of problems."

Paul took a sip from his drink. "A shack over on Winter Island, eh. I wonder if it's still there."

"Who knows? Who cares?" Frankie poured himself a draft beer. "You said you spent some time in Florida? How'd you like it? If I wasn't tied to this damn bar, that's where I'd be headed. These winters are about to do me in."

"It's pretty brutal in the summer. Humidity like you've never felt before. The winter's great. But let me tell you, you wouldn't believe where I was working. Remember those freak shows they used to have in all the carnivals when we were kids?"

"Yeah, I do. You don't see them anymore."

"That's what I thought until I started working at one. It was a creep show. That's what I'd call it. A creepy roadside attraction called Doctor Merriweather's Menagerie of Human Oddities."

The bartender leaned closer. "Human oddities?"

Paul nodded. "And that's what it was. I could tell you stories that would —"

The front door opened, and two couples walked in. A man waved. "Hi, Frankie. We told you we'd be back."

The bartender looked over and smiled. "Is the whole crew coming?"

"Yes. Eight more right behind us."

Frankie grabbed a bar rag. "Looks like you're going to have to finish your story some other time. I'm going to be real busy."

He paused. "And just let me be clear about something. I'm sure as hell not going to put up with any of your nonsense again. We're running a nice friendly place here now. I chased the riff-raff out a long time ago."

Paul pulled a few bills from his pocket and slapped them on the bar. "Like I said, you're getting me mixed up with my poor deceased friend." He stepped outside, walked to the curb, and stuck out his thumb.

*****

Harold stood outside Lillian's room at the end of the hallway on the second floor and listened as the rain beat down on the roof. He stepped away. Was this conversation necessary? He turned back to the door and knocked softly.

"Yes?" a muffled voice responded.

"It's me, Harold. Could I come in for a moment?"

There was a rustle of clothing and the door slowly opened. Lillian peeked out. "Do you need me for something?"

Harold smiled. "No, dear. Just...I thought maybe we could talk for a moment."

Lillian opened the door wider. She glanced over at the kettle sitting on a hot plate. "Can I offer you a cup of tea?"

"No thanks. I'm sorry to bother you on your day off, but...I just wanted to make sure you were all right."

"All right? What makes you think I'm not?"

Harold coughed. "Maybe it's just my imagination, but I have a feeling that you've been trying to stay away from Eric as much as possible. Is his visit bothering you for some reason?"

A quick blush flared on Lillian's cheeks. She sat down on an embroidered wingback chair. "Oh, goodness. Has it been that obvious? Has he said something?"

39

"No. He hasn't mentioned anything, but I've noticed when he comes into a room, you seem to leave quickly. There's been a bunch of little things like that since he arrived."

She smoothed a doily on the arm of the chair. "I…I suppose I have. I'm embarrassed it's been so noticeable."

Harold pulled a chair over and sat down next to her. "What's the problem? Shall I ask him to leave?"

She stiffened. "Oh, no. Please. It's just that, I know he's hurting, and there's things Claire said to me before she…" Tears welled up in her eyes.

"What kind of things?"

Lillian shook her head. "No. I'm not going to repeat them. You know Claire. When she was upset, sometimes she could blurt out things that weren't very nice." She reached over and took his hand. "I'm sorry. I'll do better. If I've offended Eric, I'll certainly apologize."

Harold stood. "No, I don't think he's even noticed. An apology isn't necessary. But I know you, Lillian. I could tell something was bothering you. Put this conversation out of your head and enjoy the rest of your day off."

He stepped out of her room and closed the door. What could Claire have told her that would make her want to avoid being around Eric?

He returned to the main floor and found his brother-in-law sitting at a desk in the library surrounded by papers. "Ready to go?"

Eric looked up. "Go? No. I'm not ready to go. I'm finally making some progress. Tell your friend the muse has finally kicked in. I'll see him some other time."

Harold motioned for him. "I'll do nothing of the sort. Knowing Brian, I'm sure he's already prepared a wonderful lunch for us. Come on. Give yourself a break. I heard you down here early. When was it, around seven?"

Eric straightened a stack of papers. "Yes. I made some coffee and started at it right after seven." He stood up. "My outline's coming together. I wasn't able to concentrate at home, but here I seem to have cleared away the cobwebs. Thank you so much for putting up with me."

"I'm not putting up with you. I'm glad you're here." He moved toward the door. "It's raining pretty hard out there. I've put two umbrellas in the car."

Harold backed his car out of the garage. They climbed steadily west on Oak Street until the road dead-ended into Summit Drive.

Eric stared out the window. "That's quite an elevation change."

Harold nodded. "With all those quick twists and turns, the road rises about six-hundred feet. Great view of the lake from here."

Two miles later, Harold slowed as they drove past the sign for Ledge Park. "This is where those trails are you were asking about."

"The book you gave me listed three. Two loop trails that go for about two miles and one shorter one that skirts the edge of the bluff. I'm eager to check them out. Maybe tomorrow or the next day if the weather clears."

"Sounds like this rain may continue through tomorrow." Harold slowed the car. "Here's where we turn to Brian's place." The car bounced down a narrow road that snaked through a dense evergreen forest. Pine, hemlock, and cedar trees grew so thick it was impossible to see through them.

Harold parked in front of a modest ranch house that seemed to be teetering on the edge of a cliff. Even through the rain-streaked window, Eric could tell the house had a magnificent view of Lake Michigan. The front door flew open and Brian appeared in the doorway holding a huge umbrella.

Harold reached into the back seat and handed Eric a much smaller one. "Look. He's ready for us. Aren't you glad you came?"

Eric gave a weak smile, took the umbrella, and stepped out from the car. It was only a few feet to the front door.

"I see you gentlemen brought your own rain gear. Come in, come in." Brian held the door open, then directed them to the living room. He came over and shook Eric's hand. "So nice of you to come. I know what Harold's drinking. What can I get for you?"

"What's Harold drinking?" Eric asked.

Brian glanced over at his friend. "Vodka martini, very dry, two olives and an onion, right?"

Harold gave a thumbs up.

"I'll have the same." Eric moved closer to the living room window. "This view is spectacular."

Brian joined him. "You can see the harbor from here. I've got a boat down there. Third from the right."

"I see it. What is it?"

"It's an eighteen-foot Glastron."

Eric followed the shoreline to the north. "Are those buildings Roy's Lakeside Cottages?"

"Yep. Still there and more decrepit than ever."

Harold walked over. "Brian, didn't you work there one summer?"

"I did. Just after high school, along with every derelict that ever came through Red Cedar Cove."

"Why's that?" Eric asked.

"Because Roy wouldn't pay hardly anything, but he'd let you stay in one of the cabins if you worked for him. It was a perfect situation for somebody who was down on their luck." Brian turned to Eric. "What made you pick them out?"

"I stayed there once when I first met Claire. I'd come to town to surprise her. There really wasn't any other place to stay."

"Still isn't," Harold added.

"They were pretty primitive then. I can't believe they're still open."

Brian said, "The problem with them now is no decent people would even consider staying there. Times have changed. People want luxury now days."

"Or cleanliness," Harold laughed. He turned back to the window. "Yes. That view's magnificent."

Brian walked over to a small bar. "Thank you. I've lived here for so long, I'm afraid I don't even notice it anymore." He busied himself making martinis and then gave one to Harold. "Here you go, my friend." He handed the other to Eric. "You live in a high rise in the middle of Chicago, don't you? I'm afraid my humble view can't compare to that."

Eric smiled. "Can't compare to the noise, congestion…" He was going to continue with crime but changed his mind.

Brian picked up his drink, which had already been made, and toasted, "Here's to good friends." Everyone lifted their glasses. Brian continued, "Harold tells me you've been slaving away on your new novel. It must be terribly daunting trying to write something new when Claire's book got such a wonderful reception. I mean the Macintosh Award. It doesn't get much better than that. I can't imagine the pressure that must put on you."

Eric tried to swallow the sip he had taken from his drink. He wasn't expecting that. "Well, it's not really something I think about. Claire had her story to tell, and I've got mine. But thanks to Harold's hospitality, I've been able to make some progress on my outline."

Brian turned to Harold. "What about your manuscript? I bet it follows your sister's tour-de-force and really shakes up the academia world."

"Let's put it this way. If I can get an eyebrow raised by one or two medieval history scholars, if I'm even lucky enough to get my manuscript published in one of our journals, I'll be happy."

Brian shook his head. "There you go. You and Claire always tried to bury your wonderful accomplishments. It's just not fair. Eric and I have to struggle just to make it through every day, but not you guys." He took a sip from his drink and turned back to Eric. "Speaking of struggle. I'm wondering why you're even bothering to write another book. I'm sure the checks from Claire's latest one are pouring in. You'll probably never have to work another day in your life." He stared off into the distance. "Such a shame. Poor Claire. Her life snuffed out right when she had achieved the pinnacle of success."

Eric turned to Harold and shot him a thin smile. This was even worse than he imagined. Why had he agreed to come? He didn't really have a choice in the matter, did he? He glanced at his watch. How was he going to endure another few hours of this?

"You guys ready for lunch? Everything's made. I just need to put out a few things." Brian disappeared into the kitchen.

There was an awkward silence. Eric wanted to tell Harold that he knew coming here was a bad idea, but he held himself back.

Harold joined him at the large living room window. "He's got one hell of a panoramic overlook, doesn't he?"

"Yes. It's magnificent. You can see the whole town from here." Eric pointed. "Is that an island out there?"

"That's Winter Island. It's about twenty acres with nothing on it but woods. The city keeps wanting to make it into a park with trails and things. You know, keep it preserved. But they can never work out a deal with the state."

Brian poked his head in. "Lunch is ready."

They followed him into the dining room where sliced beef and turkey were set out next to a pile of buns. "I bought some potato salad and picked up a macaroni salad, too. There's lettuce, onions, mustard, pickles, and mayo for your sandwiches. We've got homemade apple pie for dessert."

"You made an apple pie?" Harold asked.

Brian laughed. "No. I bought it down at the farmer's market yesterday. There's fresh coffee if you want some."

Eric spread yellow mustard on a bun. "I hear you sold the family business recently."

"I did. We had a diesel repair shop over in Trout Creek. My father started it in 1942. On one hand, I hated to let it go, but I don't have any brothers or sisters that could have taken it over. I've had a few health issues. It was time to get rid of it." He reached for a bun. "But then again, that damned family business kept me prisoner here. I wasn't able to see the world like you guys. I was born in Trout Creek and lived in this area my whole life. I used to have dreams about traveling to Europe, maybe Japan. Hell, I've never even seen a national park."

Eric glanced around. "But look what you have here. A great place with a million-dollar view. Are you enjoying your retirement?"

Brian hesitated. "I guess I am. I'm a little bored. I volunteer my mechanical services to the fire department, but that doesn't take up much of my time. There's not a whole lot to do around here. I read about all those plays and concerts that are going on in Chicago. I used to play the guitar a little. I always wanted to go see one of those great rock and roll bands there, but I was always tied to the business."

"Well, you're free now. You should visit the Windy City and take in a concert or two."

Brian shook his head. "All the rockers from my generation are either dead or too damn old to play. I missed out on all of that. Does anyone want another drink?"

"Coffee's good for me," Harold responded.

"Me too," Eric said as he held up his cup.

"You guys are light weights." Brian got up and made himself another drink. "But I did go over to the party they had for Claire when her book won the Macintosh award. I wanted Harold to go with me, but he was out of town."

"I hated to miss it," Harold said. "They didn't provide much advance notice."

"How was it?" Eric asked.

"It was sad, is what it was. With Claire dead, they almost cancelled it, but the librarian said no, it should go on. It turned out to be quite strange. Everyone was trying to figure out which one of her characters was based on somebody from Red Cedar Cove. Especially the killer."

Eric frowned. "I don't understand that. Harold mentioned something like that to me, also. I read her first draft, and I edited her manuscript. I never once thought she referenced Red Cedar Cove or anyone that lived here."

Brian leaned closer. "But you don't know these people like we do."

Chapter 7

BUDDY'S MOTHER SET down a plate with two pancakes. "Here. I can't believe you never told me about this teacher's workday until today. I have to clean a friend of Mrs. Franklin's house. If I'd known about this, I'd have made some arrangements for you. Teacher workday? Isn't their day supposed to be teaching something to the kids?"

"I did tell you, but I think you may have been sleeping in the chair. You mumbled something. I thought you heard me."

Christine grabbed a cup of coffee and sat down across from him. "I think you forgot on purpose."

Buddy shook his head. "No. I told you." He cut a piece of pancake with his fork. "Ma, I heard some crazy things last night. I think they came from that guy in the cabin next door."

His mother stared at him. "I know. I heard it too." She hesitated. "I've had a few conversations with Jack, um…Mr. McGill. He's been through a lot. He was in the army and…let's just say, he needs to rest and forget about some things."

Buddy's head snapped up. "So, I can go over there and talk to him now?"

She sipped her coffee. "Not yet. He needs peace and quiet. Maybe later, I'm not sure."

"What was he yelling about?"

She stood. "I have to leave. Don't worry about Mr. McGill. It's none of our business. What are your plans for the day? Are you going over to Darrell's house?"

Buddy nodded. "Yep. He bought a few new comics. He wants me to come over and see them."

She kissed him on the forehead. "Good. Tell his mother I said hello."

After she left, Buddy finished his breakfast and stepped outside. What he had told his mother was true. He didn't want to be a liar. It just wasn't the whole story. After reading the comics, he and Darrell planned on going over to Winter Island to put together two more walls for the tree house.

He glanced under the porch of the cabin next door. The canoe? It was gone! Buddy ran over and peered under the old wooden structure. Drag marks showed where the boat had been.

A door opened. Buddy looked up to see Mr. McGill staring down at him. "What's going on? Did your dog chase something under the porch?"

Buddy scrambled to his feet. "No. King's in the house. I'm looking for the canoe. It's always here. Did…did you take it?

"That old thing? No, I didn't take it. If I did, it would have been to the junk yard."

Buddy let out a sigh. "Then somebody stole it."

Jack smiled. "I hardly think so."

Buddy stepped toward the sidewalk. "Well, it's gone. Wait till Darrell hears about this. He's not gonna believe it."

Jack sat down on a rusted metal chair. "I'll keep my eye out for it. If I spot it somewhere, I'll let you know."

"Thanks."

Jack motioned. "Buddy, come over here for a minute."

"What?"

"Speaking of keeping an eye out, I'll keep a lookout for your canoe, but I want you to do me a favor too."

"Okay. What is it?"

"I was in town last night, and I spotted a guy who might be looking for me. If anybody comes around asking questions, tell them you don't know me, okay?"

"Ah, okay, but…you want me to lie?"

Jack folded his arms. "Well, I guess it's a lie, but sometimes a lie can lead to good things. This guy and his friends aren't very nice people. It wouldn't be a good thing if they knew I lived here."

"Okay. If anybody asks, I'll just say, 'Jack who'?"

He smiled. "That'll be good. Now you probably don't want to be telling your mom about this conversation. She…she probably wouldn't understand. This is man to man stuff."

Buddy nodded. "Yep."

Jack got up, winked, and disappeared back into the cabin.

Buddy returned to the house, pulled open the door, and called for his dog. "Come on, King. We're late."

Twenty minutes later he was standing in Darrell's bedroom. "It's gone, I tell you. Somebody stole it."

"Who the heck would take that old piece of crap? It was more patches than canoe."

"I don't know, but what are we going to do now? I thought we had the whole day to build them walls. Now we can't even get over there."

"Calm down, Buddy. My sister's boyfriend, Chuck, has a canoe. He said I can use it anytime. It's over on Pike Street."

"Great. Let's go."

"What about the comics?" Darrell asked. "I thought you wanted to see them."

Buddy ran to the door. "Later. We've got work to do."

*****

As they glided up to the island, Buddy jumped out and pulled the canoe onto the sand. "That's one sleek boat. It didn't take us long to get over here."

49

Darrell held up his paddle. "Good thing I remembered to bring this."

Buddy made sure the boat was secured and then bounded toward the woods. "Last one there's a big old booger." King barked and ran after him.

Darrell was close behind. When they got to the tree house, Buddy skidded to a stop. "What the —?"

His friend ran up behind him. "Where'd all our plywood go?"

Buddy stared at the ground. "Are you kidding me? First somebody steals the canoe, now all our wood's gone."

Darrell looked up at the huge oak branches. "At least our one lonely wall's still there."

"Maybe somebody else is gonna build a tree house, and they stole all our wood." Buddy pulled himself onto the first board they had nailed to the tree. "Let's find out."

They climbed up to the two-by-four platform and looked around.

Darrell spit and watched as it sailed toward the ground. "I don't see another tree house."

Buddy brought his hand up and shaded his eyes. "Me either. But look!" He pointed through the trees. "Smoke."

"Do you think somebody stole our wood to build a fire?"

Buddy moved over to the steps. "I hope not."

King led the way as the two boys ran down the narrow path to the other side of the island. As they neared a clearing, Buddy motioned for Darrell to slow down. "Look. That smoke's coming from the old shack."

Darrell stared up at the roof. "And there's our plywood. Somebody's patched up the holes with our stuff."

Buddy turned. "I thought you said that old hermit died?"

"That's what my dad told me."

"Looks like somebody's living there now. Your dad must be wrong. Who else would want to stay in that dump?" Buddy looked around. "Where's King?"

"He's digging in the sand near the shoreline."

Buddy turned. "Hey! There's the missing canoe."

"Well, I'll be. Whoever's in the shack must have stolen the canoe to get out here. Then he took our wood to patch up the roof."

Buddy took a step toward the cabin. "I'm gonna get our boat back."

Darrell grabbed him by the arm. "Are you nuts? Whoever's in there must be a crazy person. Nobody else would live in that crappy place. If he catches you, he'll probably feed you to the rats."

Buddy pulled free. "The boat's not his, and besides, we need it. We can't be using Chuck's boat forever. I'm gonna sneak through the woods and grab the canoe from behind the cabin."

Darrell shook his head as Buddy stepped into the forest. "You're crazy."

Buddy slowly made his way through the trees down to the shoreline. He glanced in the window. A man was sitting at the table. Buddy ducked low and snuck over to the canoe. King bounded up to him and barked. "Shhh, King."

As Buddy was pulling the boat closer to the water, the front door of the cabin swung open. A man ran out. "Hey, you little shit. Just what the hell do you think you're doing?"

Back at the clearing, Darrell froze.

Buddy looked up. "This boat ain't yours. I'm taking it back where it belongs."

The hair on King's neck stood up as the man approached. The dog maneuvered itself in front of Buddy, bared his teeth, and started growling.

51

"Hey now. Call your dog off. No need for that. Go ahead, take the canoe." He glanced over his shoulder. "I got a rowboat here I can use. I just borrowed that canoe to get over here."

Buddy pointed to the roof. "Looks like you borrowed our wood too."

Paul Sykes laughed. "Your wood? You mean the wood you scavenged off those old boats. I think I got just as much right to it as you do." He stepped toward the cabin. "Tell you what. You keep that dog in check, and I'll see what I can do to replace that plywood. I found another old boat down by the pines. There's enough wood on it for both of us."

As the man moved further away, King returned to where he had been digging. His paws were sending sand out in every direction. The dog stopped and started whining. It was a sound Buddy had never heard him make before.

Buddy bent down. "What you got there, boy? A rabbit?"

King buried his head in the deep hole he had created and pulled out a bone.

"Holy shit!" Buddy yelled.

Paul turned. "What?"

Buddy pointed. "Look what King just found."

"Damn, boy. That looks like a human leg bone!"

Chapter 8

ERIC SAT AT his favorite booth at the diner and watched as Denton stirred the heat out of his coffee.

Denton looked up and smiled. "I know. It drives people crazy. I like my coffee warm, not hot." He pulled the spoon out and set it on a paper napkin. "How was your weekend? Get any work done on that book of yours?"

Eric blew on his coffee and took a sip. Unlike Denton, he liked his hot. "As a matter of fact, I did. I got a lot of outlining finished this weekend."

"So, you're one of those plotter guys."

"I am. I have to plot out at least two-thirds of my story before I can start to write."

"Not me. I just jump right in."

"I tried that a few times. It didn't work for me." Eric thought for a moment. "Do you know Brian Jasper?"

Denton's eyebrows shot up. "Brian? Yeah, I know him."

"What can you tell me about him?"

"I know he's probably not going to ever be your best friend."

Eric smiled. "Funny you should say that. I got that same impression yesterday when Harold and I had lunch over at his house."

Denton leaned in close. "You had lunch with him? Now that surprises me. How did that little get together come to pass?"

"Harold had arranged to have lunch with him before he knew I was coming and insisted that I go with him. I knew there'd been some hard feelings when I started dating Claire, so I didn't want to go. And guess what? I was right. It was uncomfortable at times. Of course, I never said anything to

Harold, but on the way home he kind of apologized for Brian's behavior."

"I'm not surprised. Brian's a bitter man. We went to school together. We even hung around for a while after graduation. He complained that he was stuck here when Claire decided to go away to college. Brian's family was struggling with their repair business. They didn't have money to send him to any kind of college, let alone an elite one on the east coast like Claire's. After she broke up with him, I think that was even before you were in the picture, he never seemed to get over it. He dated a little, but for as long as I can remember, he's been a bachelor."

"I'm surprised Harold's still friends with him."

Denton nodded. "I know what you're saying. Me too. When Harold moved back home and took over the family homestead, Brian started showing up again. I don't think they have much in common. Brian seems to be a loner. Harold's probably the only friend he's got." He picked up a napkin and set it on his lap. "Remember the last time I saw you? It was Harold's birthday."

"I do remember."

"Were you there when Brian was giving Harold hell about being adopted? How lucky he was to have ended up in a nice respectable family that could provide him so much."

Eric looked surprised. "No. I must have missed that. Actually, I completely forgot Harold was adopted. Claire mentioned it once or twice at the most. It wasn't anything she ever thought about."

"I think Brian had a little too much to drink. Sounded like he was jealous that he hadn't been adopted into a better family than the one he had."

Eric shook his head. "Brian. What a piece of work."

The young waitress came over to the table. "You guys going to have what you always order, or will it be something new for breakfast this morning?"

Eric raised his cup. "I'll have the same. Warm this up for me, will you please?"

"Why break tradition this morning?" Denton asked.

The waitress asked him, "You need some more coffee?"

"No, Cheryl. It's finally the temperature I like."

She took a step away and then turned back. "I ordered your last book, Mr. Ballard. And your wife's too. They should be here in a few days."

"Thank you, Cheryl. You should have just asked me for copies. I could have mailed them to you when I go home."

"Thank you, but I really wanted to buy them. Will you sign your book for me when it comes in?"

Eric smiled. "Sure. I understand you're a writer too."

Her eyes got wide. "How did you know that? Well, I'm not sure the word "writer" is correct. Jotter of scribbles may be more appropriate."

"How did I know? Denton mentioned that he's been reviewing some of your stories."

She nodded. "He has. Boy, they sure need a lot of work."

Eric said, "I was thinking. Since we all write, maybe it would be fun if we met down at the library once a week and had a critique group. We each bring five pages, hand out copies, and read our selections. Then everyone can talk about what they liked and what they thought may need improving. I'm trying to work on my new book. I'd like some fresh eyes on my material."

Cheryl moved from one foot to another. "Oh, I don't know about that. I…I don't think my writing's good enough for you to spend time on it."

"What are you talking about? Denton's reading it, isn't he?"

"Yeah. You're right. Well, I guess that could be kind of fun."

Eric turned to Denton. "What do you think?"

Denton sighed. "I don't think so. It's been so long since I've written anything. I wouldn't know where to start."

Cheryl's face fell. "Really? But you're so good with your comments on my stories."

"Critiquing someone else's work is much easier than writing your own," Denton replied.

She turned to Eric. "Maybe you can talk him into it, Mr. Ballard."

"I'll try."

Cheryl went back to the kitchen.

"She sure is determined," Denton said.

Eric wanted to ask him about his writing career, but after what Harold had told him, he decided it wasn't the best time. Instead, he said, "It's nice to be able to focus again. I had to come back to Red Cedar Cove to do it. Chicago wasn't working for me."

Eric was surprised to see Harold walking quickly up to the table. He nodded at Denton. "Good morning."

"Morning, Harold. Nice to see you again."

Harold gave him a quick smile. "Ah, something's come up." He turned to Eric. "Can I have a moment of your time…outside?"

Eric asked, "Is something wrong?"

"No, not wrong. It's just something you may want to know." He turned to Denton. "I'm very sorry to interrupt. It's just that —"

"Think nothing of it." He looked over at Eric. "Go. I'll stay here and wait for our breakfasts."

"Okay." Eric followed his brother-in-law outside. "What is it?"

"You'll probably think I'm crazy, dragging you away like that, but something's come up, and I thought you'd be interested, since you write those mystery novels."

More puzzled than ever, Eric asked, "What?"

Harold explained that Brian had gotten a call from one of his friends in the fire department about a human bone some boys found on Winter Island. Brian was in the harbor getting his boat ready to go over there and had asked Harold if they would like to go along.

Eric asked, "A human bone?"

"I think it's a femur, but I'm not sure. Anyway, Brian is just about ready. If you want to go, we have to get over to the marina now."

"Okay, but I need a minute to say goodbye to Denton."

Harold took him by the arm. "You can't say anything about this. Brian said he's going to have to be careful where we moor the boat. We're really not supposed to be there. They've cordoned off the area. It's being treated as a crime scene."

"Okay. I'll tell him something came up and I have to leave. I'll be right back." Eric pushed open the door to the diner and walked over to the booth. "I'm really sorry, Denton. I have to pass on today's breakfast."

"Is everything okay?"

"Yes. It's nothing terrible. All of a sudden, Harold wants me to do something." He pulled out a ten-dollar bill. "I'm buying this morning. Give this to Cheryl for me, will you? Let's try and meet tomorrow morning."

"Okay, I guess. See you then."

*****

Brian steered the boat into a small cove about a quarter mile south of where several official police boats were moored and secured the boat. "Why don't you guys stay here? I'll see how close I can get without getting us kicked off the island. I'm hoping I can get my friend's attention without causing too many problems."

After he left, Eric asked, "A femur? Where do you think it came from?"

Harold frowned. "Who knows? Could be from someone who drowned and got washed up here." He stared over where Brian was headed. "God, I hope it isn't Barbara Sundstrom or Joyce Abrams."

"Joyce Abrams?" Eric repeated. That name sounded familiar. But from where? "Who are they?"

Harold squinted to see who Brian was talking to. "They're Red Cedar Cove's dirty little secrets."

"What?"

"They both disappeared around twenty years ago. Barbara vanished first. Then, almost a year later, Joyce went missing. Claire took it hard. She and Joyce were good friends."

Eric nodded. That's where he had heard that name before.

A small bass boat rounded the tip of the island and pulled up to the shore next to the police boats. As a man fiddled with an anchor, a young woman, with a dog on a leash, jumped out.

"Looks like they're bringing in a dog," Harold said.

"Probably not a good sign." Eric turned back to where Brian was talking to someone. After a few minutes, the conversation was over. Brian walked back to the boat.

Harold asked, "What did you find out?"

"They spotted a few more bones up around the woods near that big elm tree. All the rain we've been having may have washed some of the bank away. When they saw more bones, they decided to call in the dog lady. She's got a pretty lab. I'm surprised it wasn't a bloodhound."

"What do they think? Harold continued. "Is it one of the missing girls?"

Brian looked confused. "What missing girls?"

"Barbara and Joyce."

"Oh, them. That was a long time ago. I thought someone told me Joyce ran away. I don't know. Nobody said anything about those girls." He grabbed the anchor chain. "I think that's about all we're going to find out today."

*****

Buddy watched as his mother put on her lipstick. "Why do we have to go out with old Mister Sundstrom?"

"Because he's a nice man who wants to take us to dinner." She patted her lips with a tissue. "Don't you want to eat in a nice restaurant?"

"I'd rather go sit with Jack."

She reached over and tweaked his nose. "Unfortunately for you, that's not going to happen. I want you to be polite tonight. Watch your manners. It's not very often we get to go to a fancy restaurant."

"Maybe I could stay home and have a peanut butter sandwich."

She tussled his hair. "Very funny. I hear his car. Come on, let's go."

Buddy sat in the back seat on the ride to Trout Creek. When they pulled up to the restaurant, Roy asked his mother, "Do you like the food at D'Augustino's?"

"I've never eaten here. But I've heard it's wonderful."

Buddy leaned over the front seat. "Do they have hamburgers?"

Roy shook his head. "I don't think so. But their spaghetti with clam sauce is very good."

Buddy's nose wrinkled. He wasn't going to order that.

After they were seated, Roy ordered a bottle of wine and a soda for Buddy. "I hear you had some excitement over on the island."

Buddy winced and glanced over at his mother. "Um, I guess."

"That little excitement got Buddy grounded for the next month or so. He knew he wasn't supposed to take that canoe out in the lake. Now his friend's mother has told him he's not welcome at their house anymore, either."

Buddy wanted to say something about it wasn't even his idea to build the dumb treehouse in the first place but decided to just keep quiet.

"I hope they figure out what's going on over there soon," Roy said. "My daughter disappeared twenty years ago. When they find something like that, it gets you thinking."

Christine brought her napkin up to her face. "Oh. I'm so sorry."

"It's okay." He raised his glass. "I should never have brought it up."

Chapter 9

ERIC WAITED IN the lobby of the library for Denton and Cheryl to arrive. It had taken a little convincing to get Denton to join their writers' group. Eric hoped everything would turn out okay. It was always tricky about these kinds of groups. The chemistry had to be right at the beginning, or they would never last.

Cheryl pushed open the door. "Oh, you're here already." She looked around. "Is Denton coming?"

"He said he was."

Cheryl pointed to a wall-sized mural. "Have you seen this? I think it's fascinating. Someone made a huge diagram of the Lapeer's family tree."

Eric stepped back and admired the artwork. A painting depicted an oak tree that was over five feet high. Various branches of the Lapeer family radiated out from the rustic trunk. "The Lapeer's certainly have an impressive lineage, don't they?"

Cheryl gazed up at the top. "Can you believe Mr. Lapeer can trace his family all the way to the French and Indian Wars, and then back to French aristocracy?" She moved over to a letter that was encased in a large ornate gold frame. "It says this letter was from Benjamin Franklin to one of his relatives in France. I can't believe he has it sitting out here in the entry way."

"If you look closely, you can see it's a reproduction. I'm sure the original is under lock and key somewhere."

Cheryl pulled out her cell phone and took a picture of the mural. As she was finishing, Denton entered the lobby. "Hello, everybody. Is it picture taking time?"

She shoved the phone back into her purse. "I took a photo of Mr. Lapeer's family tree."

"Oh, that," Denton said. "He sure wants everyone to know how important his family is, doesn't he?" He smiled. "It's a little ostentatious, if you ask me."

As they entered the library, Cheryl directed them to a small table in the back of the building. "Mr. Lapeer said we could sit here. He thought it was out of the way enough not to cause a distraction for the other readers."

As if out of nowhere, the librarian appeared. "I just want to welcome you this evening. It's so exciting. I mean, when's the last time we've had two published authors sitting at a table here in the library? It's so nice to finally bring some class and culture to Red Cedar Cove."

"Now, Lyle," Denton replied, as he pulled out some papers from a worn leather briefcase. "I haven't been published for years. I'm afraid I'm not bringing much to this party."

"Don't be ridiculous. I remember coming in here before I was the librarian and seeing a whole shelf of your books. I read them all, too. We've still got them in the back. I have a mind to pull them out and have a retrospective of your writing one of these days."

Denton waved his hand. "Please don't. That would only serve to embarrass me. Nobody's read my stuff for years. It would take a lot of work to bring them up to today's standards."

Lyle turned to Eric. "We were all set to have a nice party to celebrate your wife's Macintosh award." He glanced down at the floor. "When that didn't happen, we had a small gathering in her memory."

"I heard," Eric replied. "That was very kind of you."

Lyle glanced over at Cheryl. "Well, again. Welcome. I'll let you authors do your thing. If you need me, I'll be in my office." He turned and disappeared as quickly as he had arrived.

"That was a little odd," Denton said. "You'd think we were picking this year's Pulitzer Prize for literature or something."

Cheryl said, "Did you guys see the news last night? They found a skeleton over on Winter Island."

"I think they found a femur, not a complete skeleton," Eric said.

Denton snapped his fingers. "That's where you went when you bolted from breakfast yesterday."

Cheryl turned. "You went over to the island?"

"Yes. It's a long story. We didn't see anything. I don't think we were supposed to be there." He pulled out a manila folder. "Sounds like Lyle's happy to have a little culture grace the library." He turned to Cheryl. "Before we begin, can you tell us something about yourself? How did you get interested in writing? Things like that."

"Sure. I'm taking a break from my senior year in college. I ran out of money, so I'm waitressing for a few months. I hope to go back for the spring semester. I'm majoring in creative writing and want to go on and get my Master's degree someday."

"Are you from around here?" Denton asked. "I don't remember ever seeing you in Red Cedar Cove until we met a few weeks ago in the diner."

"No. I'm not from here, but I enjoy the small-town atmosphere. People are friendly."

Denton tapped his pencil on the desktop. "Do you have any friends or relatives in the area?"

She smiled. "You're my friend, aren't you?"

"Um, sure. Of course, but Red Cedar Cove's so small and out of the way, I just wondered—"

Before he could finish, Cheryl said, "Oh, you won't believe this. I met the most interesting person today at the diner."

"Who was it?" Eric asked.

"A lady who owns a cadaver dog. They brought her in to check out the island after they found that …" She wrinkled her nose. "That bone."

Denton's eyes widened. "That is interesting. What did she have to say?"

"I don't think she can talk too much about it. But I asked her all kinds of questions about how she trained her dogs and what other kinds of cases she's been on. She was fascinating."

Denton turned to Eric. "Sounds like someone you should be talking to."

"No kidding. I'd love to pick her brain sometime."

"I think she's coming in tomorrow for breakfast. Maybe I can introduce her to you guys."

"That would be nice," Eric said.

Denton picked up his papers. "Enough stalling. Who wants to go first?"

Eric turned to Cheryl. "How about you?"

"Me? I don't know about that." She hesitated. "Oh, okay. Maybe it would be better to get it over with quickly. I don't know how I'm going to be able to compete with you pros." She handed them five pages.

"There's no competing here," Denton said. "Just honest, friendly tips and comments."

When Cheryl was finished reading, both Eric and Denton had a few suggestions where she could improve her manuscript. She scribbled down notes as they gave their advice.

Eric decided to read his pages next. When he was finished, Cheryl sat and stared down at the copy he had handed her.

"Well?" he asked.

She looked up. "Nothing. I didn't find anything I thought could be improved. I loved it."

"What about you, Denton?"

Denton smiled. "I thought it was excellent." He flipped to the second page of his copy. "I'm wondering, on the second paragraph from the top, I think you could take out the 'he saw' and write that part in more of a deep point of view."

Eric made a note. "Good idea. Anything else?"

Denton commented on a few more sections of the manuscript.

"Great input. Thank you."

"Your turn, Denton." Cheryl said.

He handed out his copies. "Be gentle, people. It's been many years since I've written anything, and from what I've just heard from both of you, I can see I'm up against some great writers."

He sat back in his chair and read his manuscript. When he finished, there was nothing but silence. He looked up. "Oh, no. Was it that bad?"

Both Eric and Cheryl were staring at him. Finally, Eric said, "I...I don't know what to say. That was brilliant!"

Cheryl wiped a tear from her eye and glanced down at his briefcase. "Did you bring other pages? I want to hear more."

"No. That's all I was able to knock out for this first meeting."

Eric smiled. "I'd say this evening was a success."

"Same time next week?" Cheryl asked.

Eric frowned. "I don't know. I'm not sure how long my brother-in-law can put up with me. You know what they say about guests and fish...."

"I hope you can make it," Denton said. "It took a little convincing, but I really liked what we were doing tonight."

They picked up their papers and walked out of the library. Cheryl and Denton had each driven to the meeting. As Eric was preparing to walk back to Harold's house, Denton asked, "Would you like a ride?"

"No. It's a beautiful night. I'm looking forward to a nice leisurely stroll."

"Do you want to meet at the diner for breakfast tomorrow?'

"Sounds good. See you then."

*****

Paul Sykes slipped behind a huge oak tree and stared at the house on the corner. There was only one light on. Was it the living room? He glanced up to the second floor. Another light could be seen at the back of the house. Damn, not a good choice. Who knew how many people were in there?

He pulled up the collar of his thin shirt and walked down the block. He stopped in front of another house. What about this place? The old Cape Cod was dark. He glanced up and down the sidewalk and then stepped closer to the porch. A newspaper leaned against the front door. At least the house wasn't abandoned.

He carefully made his way to the back door and tried the knob. It wasn't locked. He pushed the door open and stepped inside. Good ol' trusting Red Cedar Cove. Three steps led to the kitchen. He looked around. What could he use to carry what he found? A reusable grocery bag hung from a doorknob. Perfect.

He grabbed the bag and gently pulled open the bi-fold pantry door. It made a soft squeak. He stopped and glanced behind. Wait a minute. How did he not see that dog dish? It was big. Big enough for a German shepherd or husky. He turned back to the pantry and started tossing cans of food into the sack. He'd better be quick.

Shuffling footsteps approached. A light switch clicked, illuminating the room behind him.

"What's going on here?" A stooped woman with a tangled mass of white hair stood in the doorway.

Paul threw the sack over his shoulder and rushed to the back door. He eased himself out of the house and ran for the street. In the dim light, he stumbled into a dark figure on the sidewalk.

A voice called out, "Hey mister, watch where you're going. What's your hurry?"

Paul continued, even faster.

"Hey, you! Drop that bag."

The man was running after him. Paul tried to pick up his pace, but the weight of the food was slowing him down. The stranger was gaining on him. Paul dropped the sack and sprinted between two houses. He crouched down behind a thick hedge. As he struggled to catch his breath, the man stopped, bent down, and examined the contents of the bag.

Paul snuck back to a wooded area and slowly made his way to the marina. He walked over to where the rowboat was and listened. There were no sirens in the distance. What should he do? He was hungry. How long would the food on the island last? Another day? Maybe he should try a different place. No. Too damn risky. Tomorrow night. He jumped into the boat. He'd have to do a better job checking out houses.

He untied the boat and shoved off. As he rowed back to Winter Island, moonlight lit up the water. He shivered. He'd have to steal a jacket tomorrow too.

*****

As Eric entered the foyer, Lillian was standing next to an ornate entry table. She was still wearing black. "I have something for you. I…I thought it was about time you had them." She lifted several leather-bound books and handed them to him. "Here."

"What are they?"

"Claire's diaries. I found them in her bedroom when we were clearing some things out after she…was gone."

"Thank you, Lillian."

"Mr. Gustafson is in the den with Mr. Jasper. He said for you to join them if you're not too tired."

"Okay."

When Eric entered the room, Harold asked, "How'd the meeting go?"

"The meeting was great, but I had a little excitement on the way home."

"You did? What happened?"

Eric relayed his encounter with the burglar. "I returned the food to the old woman. She was a little shaken and quite upset that her dog slept through the whole thing."

"Was that Eva Thompson?" Harold asked.

"I never did get a name, but the house was on the corner of Maple and White Pine."

"Yes. That was Ms. Thompson," Brian said. "Too bad. I hope she's not too shook up. That's why I keep my doors locked at all times. People around here are still living like it's the fifties. But it's not. You just can't be too careful."

Harold glanced over at Eric and smiled. "You're right, Brian. It's not the fifties anymore. Back to the meeting, I'm anxious to hear how it went. I know you were looking forward to it."

Eric eased himself onto the couch next to Brian. "It was fun. Cheryl has real talent."

"What about old Denton? Was he able to come up with anything?"

Eric thought for a moment. "You wouldn't believe it. After he finished reading his five pages, we just sat there with our mouths hanging open. He can really write. I've got to make sure he keeps going. It's a shame how he was ostracized. Amazing how something like that could have happened back then. Anyway, they want to meet again next week, but I think I've imposed on your hospitality enough."

Harold got up and walked to the bar. "Nonsense. I'm enjoying your company. You can't leave now. We've got intrigue over on Winter Island. You've got to stay until they sort out what's going on over there. What can I get you?"

"Whiskey on the rocks, please. Speaking of that, Cheryl told us she talked to that woman we saw with the dog on the island. The woman told her all sorts of interesting stories about some of the cases she's worked on. By the way, that Lab we saw her with was a cadaver dog."

"Well, there you go," Harold replied. "You can't leave now. You need to find out more about that. It sounds like perfect information for one of your novels."

"I know."

Brian looked at the books Eric had set down. "What you got there?"

"Claire's diaries. Lillian just gave them to me."

Harold looked surprised. "Claire wrote diaries?"

"I guess so. She never told me about them."

"You're not going to read them, are you?" Brian asked.

"I don't know. If Lillian gave them to me, it's probably all right. Nobody was closer to Claire than Lillian."

69

Brian shook his head. "I don't think it's right. Those books hold thoughts Claire resumed would never see the light of day."

Harold handed Eric his drink and sat back down. "You're just worried Eric's going to see all the terrible things Claire wrote about you."

"Very funny." Brian glanced over to the doorway. "Another thing. I think it's about time Lillian starts wearing real clothes again. Those funeral dresses of hers are getting on my nerves. Harold, you need to have a talk with her."

Harold waved his hand. "It's none of my business." He looked over at Eric, "By the way, who's this Cheryl you keep mentioning?"

"She's the young waitress at the diner who's part of the writing group."

"You certainly enjoy that old diner," Harold said. "I don't know how you can eat there."

"Actually, Cheryl insisted that the three of us meet at the library, and I'm glad she did. But I have a nagging feeling something about her doesn't quite add up."

Harold's eyebrows arched. "What do you mean?"

"Denton asked her how she ended up in Red Cedar Cove. Did she have any friends or family here? I got the feeling, now I may be wrong, that she ducked his questions."

Brian shook his head. "Why would a young woman with no friends or relatives here end up waitressing at Lucy's Diner? Why not go to Trout Creek or someplace where there's things for young people to do?"

Eric tapped his finger on the arm of the chair. "That's exactly what I was wondering."

Chapter 10

THE NEXT MORNING, as Eric slid into the booth at Lucy's Diner, Denton said, "I'm still surprised at what a good time I had last night. It's been so long since I've written, I wasn't sure I'd be able to come up with five pages of anything."

"You came up with something amazing. Did you see how Cheryl was looking to see if you had more to read? Now that's the sign of great writing." He noticed two cups of coffee on the table. "Is this one for me?"

"Yes. I told her to bring two. You're always on time."

Eric took a sip. "Something crazy happened on the walk back to Harold's house last night."

"Really?"

Eric retold his run-in with the thief.

Denton leaned back. "Are you kidding? You could have been killed. You said the corner of Maple and White Pine? Was that the old Thompson place?"

"That's what Harold said."

"And you only saw food in the bag? I'm surprised. I would think Mrs. Thompson would have quite the stash of valuables." Denton thought for a moment. "Doesn't she have a big Doberman?"

"She does. It slept through the whole thing."

Cheryl walked up. A woman stood next to her. "Guys, this is the lady I was telling you about last night. The lady with the dog." She turned to the woman. "That's Denton Morris, and this is Eric Ballard."

The woman smiled. "Nice to meet you both. I'm Maxie Gray."

71

Denton, who was closer, jumped up from his seat. "Please join us. Cheryl told us about the interesting conversation you had with her. We were hoping we could meet you."

Maxie slid into the booth. "Thank you. Cheryl tells me you're both writers." She glanced over at Eric. "I'm sorry to hear about your wife, Mr. Ballard. I saw it on the news."

Eric nodded. "Thanks."

"Eric's the real author in the group," Denton said. "I used to write a long time ago."

"My father was a frustrated author. He loved to write, but he never seemed to be able to finish anything. He was a much better musician than writer. He played trumpet in a band for years." Maxie turned to Cheryl. "Could I get a cup of coffee?

Cheryl tapped a pencil on her order pad. "Is everyone having breakfast?"

When all the orders were taken, Eric said, "I was on the island when you showed up with your dog."

"You were?"

"Not officially. I accompanied a friend. How's the investigation going?"

Maxie hesitated. "Well, I can't say too much, but I think an announcement may be coming this afternoon."

"Where's your dog?" Denton asked.

"She's back at the motel in Trout Creek with another member of the team. Not sure if we're needed today."

"I was surprised to see your dog was a Lab. I would think they'd use a bloodhound for something like that," Eric said.

"Not really. Bloodhounds are great at tracking all different kinds of smells. Every person has a different scent. For cadaver work, you need a dog who can concentrate. A dog who likes doing it. My Lab's been trained on several forms of

72

decomposition." She looked around. "Probably not the best discussion just before breakfast."

"You said you thought there'd be an announcement today?" Eric asked. "My brother-in-law told me two girls disappeared from here about twenty years ago. Is it one of them?"

Denton snapped his fingers. "Barbara Sundstrom. Then about a year later Joyce Abrams went missing. Is Eric right? Is it one of them?"

Maxie sighed. "I don't really know what they've determined. I'll find out the same time as everyone else. I just heard something was coming out soon."

Does that mean your work is finished?"

"Probably not."

"I'd really like to pick your brain sometime," Eric said. "Your information would be perfect for putting in a mystery novel someday."

She laughed. "How about this? I'll trade you some of my stories for an autographed novel I can give my Dad."

"You got yourself a deal, but I'll have to mail you one. I'm staying with a friend. All my books are back in Chicago."

As Cheryl appeared with everyone's breakfast, Maxie said, "Do you guys know of a place to stay here in town? I'm getting tired of that drive from Trout Creek."

"We've got one of those bed and breakfast places," Denton replied. "But I doubt they'd take a dog." He picked up a piece of bacon. "The only other place I know of is the Lakeside Cabins, but I don't think I'd recommend them."

"Why not?" Maxie asked.

"They're a little outdated." He paused. "Probably a lot outdated."

"Are they clean?" Maxie asked.

"I couldn't say. You'd have to check them out for yourself."

"Maybe I'll do that after we're finished here."

*****

At four o'clock when Buddy got home from school, he made himself a snack, grabbed a comic book, and sat outside on the porch. After twenty minutes he threw the book down and got up from a rusted metal chair. He was bored. He'd read and reread all the comic books Jack had given him. He missed his friend Darrell.

He glanced over at the canoe that was chained to a post next door. He wouldn't be using that for a while. Probably never.

A door opened and Jack stepped out. He sat down, shook out a cigarette, and lit it. After exhaling a long plume of smoke, he looked over. "You sure have been hanging around the house a lot lately. Every time I look outside, I see you."

"No kidding. Ma wasn't very happy when she heard about me and Darrell going over to the island. Neither was Darrell's mom. I'm not allowed to play with him anymore." He kicked at the comic book. "It wasn't even my idea to build that stupid tree house. Darrell thought it would be fun."

"That's a damn shame," Jack replied. "They should be treating you guys as heroes for what you found over there. Who knows what that might lead to?"

Buddy moved closer to the railing. "No kidding. Ever since King found that bone, we've heard all kinds of stories about those girls who went missing. I hope that bone isn't from one of them, but it's got to be from something pretty important." He noticed something sitting on Jack's railing. "What's that?"

Jack looked down at a pair of binoculars. He picked them up. "What? These?"

"Yeah."

"Binoculars. You want to try them?"

Buddy smiled. "Sure. I used to have a toy set, but you could hardly see through them."

"I don't think you'll have that problem with these."

Buddy dashed over to Jack's porch. Jack handed them to him. Buddy put them to his eyes and focused with the turning knob. "Wow! I can see all the way over to the island. I...I can even see where we're building a tree house. We got a few boards nailed up and I can see them from here!" He lowered them from his eyes. "Where'd you get them?"

"Afghanistan. I picked up a pretty good pair when I was over there."

"You sure did. I've never seen any that worked this good."

Jack looked over at Buddy's cabin. "Is your mother home?"

He nodded. "She's in the kitchen."

"Can I ask you something?"

"What?"

Jack pushed himself up from the chair and stepped over to his railing. "Is your mother going out with that old guy that owns these cabins?"

Buddy felt his face flush. "No. He just takes us to dinner sometimes."

Jack took another drag from his cigarette. "You think it would be okay if you and your mom went out to eat with me one of these days?"

Buddy smiled. "Yeah. I think that would be great." He thought for a moment. "But I don't want to go to that crappy D'Augustino's place again."

"Why's that?"

"Too fancy, and they don't have anything I like on the menu."

Buddy's mother stepped out. "Buddy, they just said on TV there's going to be an announcement from the Sheriff about what they found over on the island. Come in and listen to it with me." She noticed Jack and gave him a wave.

Jack tossed his cigarette butt to the ground. "They're making an announcement?"

"Yes. Would you like to come over and hear it with us?"

"Sure."

As they sat around the television, Jack turned to Christine. "I was wondering if you guys had dinner plans tonight."

"What?"

"Dinner plans? I'm headed over to Trout Creek in a bit. I was wondering if you and Buddy would like to come with me."

Christine glanced down at her blouse. "I...I've got a stack of dishes in the sink, and I'm not really dressed to go out in public."

Buddy wanted to say something, but he knew it would be better if he stayed quiet.

"We're talking Trout Creek, not New York City. It's only Flanagan's Bar. They've got really good home cooking."

She turned back to the TV. "Here's the announcement."

A man stepped up to a microphone and said that he was the spokesperson for the county Sheriff's Department. "I know everyone in the community has been wondering about the femur that was recently discovered on Winter Island. I'm happy to confirm that our initial speculation has been validated. Doctor Daniel Moore, a forensic anthropologist from the University of Michigan, has confirmed the bone that was found was not from a recent crime. Based on the color and condition, we believe it came from a Paleo-Indian who probably died hundreds of years before Christopher Columbus discovered America. Precise dating will take at least a month, but Doctor Moore is ninety-nine percent certain the remains were not the result of a crime that occurred in modern times." He took a deep breath and surveyed the small crowd. "Are there any questions?"

A reporter shouted, "So, you're saying that this bone has nothing to do with the two local women who disappeared twenty years ago?"

"Yes. That is correct."

"What can you tell us about those cases? Are they still open?"

"Unfortunately, I don't have anything new to report on them. Yes, they remain open. Hopefully, with this new attention shining light on them, someone will come forward with a tip we can follow up on. Thank you." He turned from the podium.

Christine switched off the television. "Well, that's that."

Jack said, "I would imagine that's a huge disappointment for the community. No closure for the families of the missing girls."

Christine let out a big sigh. "Did you know one of the girls was Roy's daughter?"

Jack sat back. "Roy? The guy who owns this place?"

Christine nodded. "Yes."

"Well, I'll be."

She stood. "If you can give me a few minutes to change and put some make-up on, we'll be happy to go with you for dinner." She grabbed Buddy by the shoulder. "Come on. You need to wash up. Put on that nice shirt I bought you for Easter."

Chapter 11

HAROLD AND ERIC retired to the library after a magnificent dinner. "Lillian's outdone herself again tonight," Eric said. "You're lucky to have her."

"She's a real gem." Harold opened a humidor and picked out a cigar. "Can I interest you in a Montecristo Robusto?"

Eric shook his head. "No thanks."

"It's a great cigar. They're from Nicaragua. Brian loves them."

Eric grinned. "I'm sure it's wonderful, but I'm afraid I'd end up in the bathroom if I tried to smoke one. I never developed the habit. I wouldn't want to waste it. They sound expensive."

Lillian appeared in the doorway. "There's a young woman here to see Eric."

Harold's eyes widened. "A young woman?"

Eric asked, "Who is she?"

"Cheryl Foster."

Harold puffed on his cigar. "Who's that?"

"It's the waitress from the diner I told you about. The girl from the writing group. Why would she want to come here?"

Harold turned to Lillian. "Well, show her in for goodness sake."

Lillian disappeared into the hallway. "You did want to see her, didn't you?" Harold asked.

"I...I guess so. But I can't understand what would be so urgent that she had to come over here. She sees me every morning down at the diner."

As Lillian escorted Cheryl into the library, Cheryl gazed around the room. She spotted Eric and slowly approached. "I'm so sorry to bother you, Mr. Ballard, but…I needed someone to talk to."

Harold stepped closer and reached out his hand. "I'm Harold Gustafson, Eric's brother-in-law. I'm going to let you two talk in private."

When Harold left the room, Eric motioned for her to take a seat. "This is a surprise. What's on your mind?"

"What a beautiful library." She glanced down toward the floor. "I'm not sure this was a good idea, bothering you like this."

"Cheryl, you're not bothering me. If you have something you'd like to talk about, let's talk."

She coughed and straightened her skirt. "I noticed last night, when Denton asked me how I happened to pick Red Cedar Cove to find a place to work, you seemed to be a little skeptical about my answer."

Eric smiled. "Was I that transparent?"

"Maybe not. Maybe it was just me feeling guilty because I didn't have a very good answer to his question."

"Okay. And you've got a better one now?"

"I do, but it's pretty long."

Eric glanced at the clock. "Take your time. I don't have anywhere to go."

She took a deep breath. "Here goes. My mother and I don't have a great relationship. I was living with my stepfather before I left for college. She married him when she was twenty. I was four years old."

"So, your mother was only sixteen when she had you."

Cheryl nodded. "Yes. They divorced a few years ago. Anyway, since I was around eight years old, I tried to find out about my real dad. For some reason, even though I asked her many times, begged her even, she never told me who he was or anything about my past. I never met any aunts, uncles, or cousins, like so many of my friends had. Everything was a mystery until a few months ago when my college roommate and I decided, on a whim, to do one of those DNA kit things." She paused.

"A DNA kit? Interesting. I don't want to interrupt, but would you like a glass of wine or something?"

She smiled. "You read my mind. Yes. I'd love a glass of white, if you have any. Maybe that will help calm my nerves."

Eric walked to the bar, poured two glasses, and handed one to her. "Here. Sorry, please go on."

She took a sip. "When the results came back, the test showed I had a very good possibility of being related to someone from Red Cedar Cove. Since I lived in Ohio, I'd never heard of the place, so I looked it up."

A thought flashed through Eric's mind. Was she related to Harold somehow? He asked, "Who did it think you were related to?"

"Lyle Lapeer."

Eric set down his drink. "Really?"

"Yes. You can only imagine; I was quite excited once I did some research on the Lapeer family. After about a month, I worked up my courage and sent him a letter introducing myself."

"And?"

"Nothing. I sent another one, and when that was ignored. One afternoon I had a few drinks with my roommate. She convinced me to call him up." As she took another sip of wine, tears formed in the corner of her eyes.

Eric waited.

"He wasn't very nice. He told me he didn't know what I was talking about and to please never call him again. I was hurt, but after a while, I got kind of mad. I thought it was rude of him to

80

just brush me off when he's never even met me. The more I thought of it, I wanted to see him in person. That's what brought me to Red Cedar Cove. I didn't have any money, so I took a job at the diner."

"And did you ever meet him in person?"

She thought for a moment. "Meet him? No. I stopped in the library a few times and saw him. I just couldn't bring myself to say anything. He hadn't been exactly friendly on the phone." She glanced down. "I have something to confess."

Eric looked over. "Okay?"

"One of the reasons I was pushing for us to meet in the library, was that it would give me an excuse to go there and see him. Even if I never said anything, I thought it would be a good idea to hang around and maybe have him get to know me in a totally different way."

Eric sat quietly for a few moments. "I'm wondering…you know how impressed Mr. Lapeer is about his family's heritage. Just look at that big family tree he had painted in the library entryway. I would think that hearing from you, out of the blue like that, maybe was quite a shock to him. It didn't fit the cultured background he's spent so much time investigating. Maybe he just needs some time to digest the fact that there's a relative out there he had no idea existed."

"Maybe. But what should I do?"

"I don't really know. Let me ask you something. When we had our meeting, did Lyle have any idea you were the girl who sent him the letters and made the phone call?"

"I don't think so. He didn't let on that he did. But he could have recognized my voice."

"What's your mother's maiden name? Does she have relatives around here?"

"She told me her name was Johnson, but I think she lied. Could she have picked a more common name?"

"What about Smith?" Eric said with a smile.

"Yeah, that would have been about the same." She glanced at the clock. "I should be going. I've taken enough of your time." She stood. "Please don't mention this conversation to anyone, not even Denton. Maybe I should just go back home. If only Mr. Lapeer could get to know me."

Eric walked with her to the door. "Let me think about this for a while. Maybe we can figure something out. Don't go home yet."

She gave him a quick hug. "Thank you. You've been so kind to listen to me blabber on." She stepped out to the porch and paused. "Oh, I almost forgot. Maxie told me to tell you she's moving from Trout Creek. She's rented one of those cabins you guys told her about. She said she'd be there around ten in the morning if you wanted to come over and hear about her dog."

"Ten? I could go right after breakfast. Maybe Denton would like to come too. Thanks for remembering."

Cheryl turned and walked down to the sidewalk.

Harold was waiting for him in the library when Eric returned. "What was that all about?"

Eric shook his head. "Amazing what you can get yourself into. It's nothing, really. One of the things she wanted me to know was that the woman we saw on Winter Island with the dog will be at Lakeside Cottages tomorrow morning. I asked her if I could pick her brain like you suggested. She wants one of my books, but I don't have any with me."

"I do."

Eric turned in surprised. "You do?"

"Remember when you did that charity book signing for me a few years ago?"

Eric thought. "Yes. That was right before Claire's first book got published."

"Well, you had a few books leftover, and you told me to keep them here. I'm sure Lillian knows where they are. How many do you need?"

"Just one. That's great. I won't have to try and remember to mail one out when I get back to Chicago."

*****

Lyle Lapeer pulled his keys out of his pocket and reached for the light switch. It was ten minutes after nine. He had chased out the few regulars at eight-thirty. Now it was time to lock up. He sensed someone was behind him. As he slowly turned, a man stepped out of the shadows.

"Hello, Uncle Lyle. It's been a long time."

Lyle pulled his hand away from the switch. "What are you doing here?"

"I'm a little down on my luck. I thought maybe you could help me out a bit."

"What's wrong? Is carnival season coming to a close? I thought those shows moved down south when it started getting cold up north."

"I was down south. I'm here now."

"Get out of here. I've helped you enough. Every few years you show up for a day or two looking for a handout. What's wrong with your mother? Is she tired of bailing you out too? How old are you now, Paul? Forty-five?" Lyle didn't wait for an answer. "And still asking for handouts? Where's your pride?"

"My pride? I don't have any. There's no pride left in the family after you sucked it all out. Mother? I haven't seen her in years. The last time I was in Chicago, she was on oxygen. Her emphysema had gotten worse." He stepped closer. "So, can you help me out or what?"

Lyle pulled out his wallet and handed Paul two twenty-dollar bills. "Here. This should be enough to get you a bus ticket somewhere."

Paul smiled. "Always with the bus tickets. Never a 'Come over to the house for supper.' Or 'let's go have a drink together'. No. I get the feeling you never want your sister's bastard child hanging around smudging up your blue-blooded pedigree."

Lyle switched off the lights. "Get the hell out of here."

*****

The next morning after breakfast at the diner, Eric said, "Denton, I'm going to walk over to Lakeshore cabins. That lady with the cadaver dog is staying there. Remember she told me she'd share some experiences if I traded her a book. Why don't you come with me?"

Denton's eyes got wide. "What? You want me to go listen to stories about a dog finding decaying bodies? You don't think I have better things to do than that?"

Eric laughed. "It will be interesting. Come on. Think about the reality you'll be able to add to your writing."

"Man, you're out of your mind. I used to write adventure books for young boys. If I put anything like that in there, I'd have been in real trouble."

Eric stood up. "Come on. Just walk with me."

Denton slid out from the booth. "I must be crazy."

As they approached the motel, Maxie had already pulled up to cabin number two and was unloading things from her car.

"Can we give you a hand?" Eric asked.

She turned. "Oh, hello. Yes. If you could take this bag and that box on the seat, I'll grab Dolly."

As Eric picked up the bag and stepped toward the building, Maxie guided the Lab out from the car. "Here you go, Dolly. We've got a new home for the next few days." Maxie followed Eric into the cabin and looked around. "Quaint. I guess that's the best word I can think of to describe it."

Denton asked, "Where do you want this box?"

"Just set it over next to the table."

Eric looked around. "I stayed here years ago. It doesn't seem like they've changed a thing."

Denton reached out to pet the dog. "Is it okay?"

"Sure. Dolly loves attention when she's not working."

Eric held out a book.

"What's this?"

"You asked me to bring a book, but I told you I'd have to mail you one. I'm staying with my brother-in-law. He found this copy for me."

She smiled. "Oh, thank you. I'm going to read it first and then give it to my Dad."

She picked up a large glass ashtray. "Denton, you were right. It's quite dated, but I don't mind. It's clean, the linens are fresh, and my dog isn't a problem. That's everything I was looking for." She motioned toward a worn couch. "Sit down." She glanced over at Eric. "If I remember correctly, I owe you a few of my experiences in exchange for this book."

"You do."

After the first few stories, Denton glared at Eric and then stood up. "I'm sorry, but...I got something to do. Please excuse me." He bent down close to Eric and whispered, "I'm gonna get you for this." He walked to the door and almost ran down the porch steps.

Eric turned to Maxie. "Please excuse my friend. I don't think he could take any more. It's my fault. I made him come with me."

She laughed. "Was I too explicit? I'm sorry. I'll tone down some of the descriptions."

Eric shook his head. "No. Please, these are the details I need to know about."

"Okay. If you insist." Maxie continued to entertain Eric with some fascinating, and some very disturbing experiences she had encountered about finding corpses around the country. He wished he had brought a notebook.

After an especially morbid tale, Dolly started whimpering and looked toward the door. Maxie reached for the dog's leash. "I need to take her out."

"I'll come with you."

They walked down the porch steps, and Dolly immediately found a spot to do her business.

"I have to hand it to you," Eric said. "I don't know if I could have stomached some of the things you told me about. Does...does it ever bother you? Do you have nightmares about what you've discovered?"

"It was tough at first. I must admit there were times at the beginning that I thought I couldn't do it. But then I'd see the look on the relatives faces. The relief that their loved ones had been found. Of course, they were saddened, but they didn't have to wonder anymore. I wish you could see some of the wonderful letters and cards I've received the last few years. That's what keeps me going." She reached down and petted Dolly's head. "I'd like to take her for a little walk. Do you mind?"

"No. It's so nice out. That would be fine."

They made their way down to the water's edge and followed the shoreline. Maxie unclipped the leash.

Eric glanced over at Maxie's hand and noticed she wasn't wearing a wedding band. "What does your boyfriend think of you doing this?"

She turned. "What boyfriend?"

"Oh. I don't know. I just presumed that you —"

"I haven't had a boyfriend for about a year now. Let's just say, he enjoyed the money I was bringing in. So much so, he didn't think he needed to find a job. I got tired of that real quick."

"I can imagine."

They walked for another twenty minutes, and then Maxie said, "Maybe we should be getting back."

As they neared the cabins, a boy called out from a porch next to Maxie's place. "Hey, Lady. Is that the dog that was searching the island?"

She called Dolly over and snapped the leash back on. "It is. How did you know that?"

"I saw you guys on TV. I'm the kid that found the bone. Can I pet your dog?"

They walked closer. "Sure. So you found the bone, did you?"

"Well, my dog did." Buddy ran down from the porch.

"What kind of dog do you have?" Eric asked.

"A big German shepherd named King. He's in the house. Do you want to see him?"

Maxie stopped. "Ah, maybe some other time." She glanced over at Dolly.

Dolly's head was up sniffing the air. She started pulling on the leash.

"What's the matter?" Eric asked. "Does she want to go back home?"

Maxie was staring at the dog. "No. Dolly's indicating that she's caught a whiff of something." Maxie bent down. "What is it, girl?"

The dog continued to pull. Maxie took a few steps and followed. The dog circled around to the back of the cabin, wined, and then sat down.

Eric could see something was concerning Maxie. "What's going on?"

"I...I'm not sure. She's indicating that something's here." Maxie tried to pull on the leash, but the dog wouldn't budge.

"Here?" Eric asked. "What could be here?"

Maxie reached into her pocket and handed Eric her car keys. "I don't know, but I need to check this out. Could you run over to my car and pull out a metal probe and shovel I've got in the trunk?"

He took the keys. "Sure."

Buddy had followed them to the back of the cabin. When Eric returned, Buddy pointed to the tools. "What are those for?"

Maxie said, "I want you to stay back a ways, okay? I just need to poke around here for a few minutes." She turned to Eric. "I don't think this is anything, but keep a watch on that kid, just in case."

"Okay."

Maxie stepped over to the side of the cabin, where the dog was sitting. "Okay, Dolly. It's okay." She took the long metal probe and stuck it in the ground a few times. After sinking into the dirt and hitting a few stones, Maxie moved it about a foot and plunged it into the soil again. She poked the soft ground several times and then reached for the shovel.

"Can I help you?" Eric asked.

She shook her head. "No." She continued to dig down about two feet. The shovel collided with something. Maxie stopped, scraped away some loose soil, and bent down. She dropped to her knees and started scooping out handfuls of sand.

After a few minutes she motioned for Eric. "I need you to make sure that kid goes back inside the cabin. Tell him to keep his dog inside. You need to get over to my place and bring me my purse. I need my cell phone. Now."

"What is it?"

"I'm not sure, but we need to call the authorities."

Eric walked over to the boy. "What did you say your name was?"

"Buddy."

"Is your mother home?"

"Yeah. Why?"

"I need you to go in the house. Don't ask me any questions, because I don't really have any answers."

Twenty minutes later, a police officer appeared at the back of the cabin. "What's going on, Maxie? I got a call you wanted me to stop by."

She pointed to the ground. "Dolly registered a scent. I dug around a little, and I think I've found something. Looks like bone to me. I didn't want to disturb the scene, so I called in and asked if you could come by."

He stepped closer to the hole and peered down. "Are you sure?"

"I've done this more than a few times, Bob. Dolly's pretty reliable. Yeah. Something's down there. I just don't know what."

Officer Meyer pulled out his police radio. "Well, let's find out."

Chapter 12

ROY SUNDSTROM RAN out of the office as a line of police cars and a white van pulled up to his property. He approached an officer. "What the hell's going on?"

"We're checking out something that was found behind one of your cabins."

"Oh, you are? What did you find? This is my place. You'd think you'd have the courtesy to come and tell me what's happening." He followed the policeman to the back of Cabin number three.

A line of yellow tape had already been strung around the back of the building. The officer pointed toward the cabin. "Those people staying in there, you need to move them."

"Move them? To where? Why do I have to move them? They've been there for a month already. What the hell have they done?" He turned toward the cabin. "Wait a minute. Is it that kid? Has he done something? Isn't he the one who found that bone on the island? Just what the hell's going on back here?"

"Mr. Sundstrom, someone will be over to talk to you when we know a little more. Right now, I need you to move those people out of this cabin. Do you understand?"

Roy took a step back. "I guess." He walked away shaking his head.

Eric, Maxie, and the dog had been moved behind the yellow tape. They watched as a forensic team started to examine the area.

After half an hour, one of the people digging yelled, "We got something here. Joe, you need to set up the tent. Get everyone to the front of the cabin and keep them out of here."

The man named Joe spoke to several of the officers and then walked over to a van.

"Okay, folks. You heard the man. We all need to move away from here."

Roy ran up to the yellow line. "What is it? What have you found?" He was sweating heavily.

"We're not sure yet, Mr. Sundstrom. But we have to make room for these people to work."

Roy watched as three men began setting up a white tent. "What the hell's that for?" He grabbed the cop. "Dammit. What's going on? I need to know. What's buried back there? I got a missing —"

Eric stepped over. "You need to calm down. Let the man do his job. Come on. We're leaving them to their business. Walk with us."

Roy let go his grip and slowly followed Eric, Maxie, and the dog to the front of the cabin.

An hour later a detective dressed in a blue suit and red tie walked up to them. "Mr. Sundstrom, I'm detective Wolf. Would you come with me, please?"

"What is it? What did you find back there?"

"Is there a place we can talk privately? Your office, perhaps?"

As they retreated, Eric asked Maxie, "What do you think that was all about?"

She grimaced. "Probably nothing good."

Roy's hand shook as he handed the detective a cup of coffee. "Please don't tell me you've found...my daughter."

Detective Wolf took the cup and leaned back in his chair. "I'm not sure if it's your daughter or not, but we've definitely found human remains. I'm familiar with your daughter's case.

In fact, I just reviewed it about a week ago. Could you tell me what you remember about her disappearance?"

Roy leaned over and rested his head in his hands. "Dear God. This is the day I've dreaded ever since Barb went missing. But how? How did she end up there?"

"Like I mentioned, Mr. Sundstrom, we haven't identified anybody yet."

Roy looked up. "I'm sure you're trying to be kind and all, but..." He took a few deep breaths. "Anyway, Barb was sixteen when she went missing. I'd been separated from my wife for about a year. I just presumed Barb had gone over to her house to stay for a while like she usually did. We'd had a fight."

"With your daughter or your wife?"

"My daughter. We were having plenty of arguments at that time. You know, her being a smart-mouthed teenager."

"What were the fights about?"

Roy pushed away his coffee. "What weren't they about? Everything, I guess. Her curfew, the clothes she wore, all the boys that were coming around, her grades."

"So what happened when she disappeared?"

"It got to be late, about midnight. It was a school night, and she was supposed to be home by ten o'clock. I called her mother just after twelve, to make sure Barb was there. She said she wasn't. We talked a bit. She thought she was probably staying at one of her girlfriends. Since it was so late, we decided to wait 'till morning and make sure she made it to school."

"You didn't make any other calls that night?"

"No. But the next morning, my wife called and told me Barb hadn't made it to her first class. June had called around to her friends, but nobody had seen her. That's when we decided to call you guys."

"Your wife is now deceased, correct?"

Roy nodded. "Yeah. We got a divorce about a year after Barb disappeared. June started drinking a lot. She got hit by a car in Trout Creek fifteen years ago. She was coming out of the Whitefish Pub drunk as a skunk. The poor guy who hit her didn't get charged. A hell of a thing to live with." Roy's shoulders slumped. "God, if that's Barb back there, I envy June. She doesn't have to live with this."

*****

Jack set down a cardboard box on the floor of Cabin number one. "I think this is the last of it."

Christine threw herself onto the worn couch. "Thank you so much for your help." She closed her eyes for a second. "I can't believe this. Poor Buddy. First he finds a human bone on that island, then they find a body under our cabin. Can you believe it? Our cabin!" She looked over at him. "Can I have a cigarette? Shit. I quit three years ago, but I really want one."

Jack pulled out his pack and handed it to her.

"Thanks for letting him watch TV over at your place."

"You'll have to keep an eye on him. He may need some counseling."

"Counseling? I don't have any money for something like that."

Jack stood. "I've got a bottle of wine. Let me get it." He pushed open the door and stopped. "By the way, you wouldn't have to pay for it. I know who to talk to." He smiled. "God knows I've had enough therapy."

Christine lit her cigarette. She was wondering what he meant by that, when he returned with the wine and two paper cups.

He poured them each some wine and handed one to her. "I'm sure you were trying to figure out what I meant by that last statement."

She took a sip. "Ah…yes. I have to admit I was."

He settled onto the couch next to her. "When I came back from Afghanistan, I thought everything was fine. I was so happy to be home. But it didn't take long before things were not just fine. Of course, I didn't see it at first. But my wife, my friends, and my parents saw it. After a couple of bad years and a nasty divorce, I went to the VA and started getting counseling. It helped. I wouldn't say I'm one hundred percent back to normal, but I'm probably better than seventy-five percent."

"How did you get here? To a cabin in Red Cedar Cove?"

"I was living with a friend in Grand Rapids. It wasn't a good environment. I used to come up here fishing a lot before the army. I remembered this place, these cottages, and how peaceful it is—" He stopped. "Or was. Anyway, that's my story. I still go to counseling. I know who to talk to if you think Buddy needs some help."

"Thank you. I'll keep an eye on him and see how he does in the next few days." She gave a slight shiver. "Just the thought of it. That girl right under our floor. Gone for so many years."

"What do you think happened?"

"I have no idea. I heard that two girls had gone missing. I think there was about a year between each of their disappearances. But I'm not from here, so I never got much of the story."

Jack refilled his glass. "Me either. Just what I saw on TV. But we were younger back then. What did we know about the world?"

"When that happened, I can't remember which one, but I can still hear my mother taking me in the house and giving me a lecture about having to be careful. That there were bad people out there who could take you."

"It's just hard to believe that right here in Red Cedar Cove, something like that could happen. And happen twice."

A sharp knock at the door startled Christine. She put her wine down and peered out the window. "It's Roy." She opened the door.

"I was just making sure you got moved and settled in okay." He glanced inside. "What's he doing there?"

Somewhat surprised at Roy's tone, Christine said, "He was nice enough to help me move."

Roy lowered his voice and stepped closer. "You might want to be careful with that one. From what I hear, he's got some issues."

"Don't we all, Roy. Don't we all."

As Roy turned and stepped away, he muttered, "Maybe, But some of us more than others."

*****

The next morning Harold walked up to Eric. "Lillian tells me you're leaving this morning. Is that true?"

"Yes. We talked about this last night."

"I know, but I thought I'd convinced you into staying a few more days."

"It's been a whole week already. It's done me good to get away. I've made some good progress on my book thanks to the serenity of your magnificent library, and the necessity of having something to have written for that writer's group, but enough is enough. I don't want to take advantage of your hospitality."

Harold shook his head. "Why leave now when you're right in the thick of it. They just found that body over at the cabins.

Can it get any more interesting than that for a mystery writer? Think about it, now's not the time to go."

"Don't tempt me, Harold. You'll have to keep me informed. I'm headed over to the diner for one last breakfast with Denton. Why don't you come with me?"

Harold winced. "That greasy spoon? Oh, okay. Maybe Denton can talk some sense into you when we're there."

Denton was already sitting in the booth when they arrived. "Looks like you've brought a guest with you this morning. Welcome, Harold. Here, sit down next to me."

Harold slid into the booth. "Did you know Eric's heading back to Chicago once we're done here?"

Denton nodded. "I did. Both Cheryl and I tried to change his mind, but he made it clear that he didn't want to overstay his welcome."

Harold's eyes widened. "Overstay his welcome?" He turned to Eric. "Oh, come on. You know better than that."

"Enough you two. Here comes Cheryl. Figure out what you want to order."

*****

Lillian was heading up the stairs on her way to strip the linens from Eric's bed, when she heard a noise behind the closed door. Was Eric still there? No. She saw them both head out on their way to the diner. She stopped. Someone definitely was moving around inside. She slowly approached the room and pushed the door open a few inches. A man was rifling through the dresser drawers. She yelled, "Hey! What are you doing in here?"

He turned. His face was obscured by a knitted ski mask.

As she backed away from the door, he grabbed something and rushed at her as he made his way to the staircase. She tried to push him away, but he was too strong. He rammed her with his shoulder. She fell to her knees and rolled to the edge of the stairway. Her head slammed into an ornate oak spindle. Lillian tried to grab onto the carpet but there was nothing to hang on to. She let out a scream and tumbled down the stairs.

*****

On the walk back to the house, Harold said, "I guess I'm not the only one who's upset about you heading back to Chicago. That fledgling writer's group wasn't very happy that you're leaving either."

Eric stopped and grabbed his brother-in-law by the arm. "Harold, look. There's a police car and ambulance pulled up to your house."

"What the hell?"

They ran up the hill and stopped in front of a uniformed officer. "This is my house. What's going on?" Harold asked.

"You've had a break-in. The perpetrator pushed your housekeeper down the stairs. She's suffered a broken arm. There may be more internal injuries. They're taking her to the hospital now to check her out."

Harold ran over to the ambulance where Lillian was lying inside on a gurney. "Are you okay? What happened?"

She slowly turned her head. "Oh, Harold. It was awful. After you left, I went upstairs to start working on Eric's room. I heard a noise. A man was looking through the dresser drawers. When he spotted me, he ran straight at me and pushed me away. I lost my balance and fell down the stairs. They tell me I've broken my arm."

James R. Nelson

A medic appeared and took hold of the back door. "Sorry. I'm going to have to close this now. We're headed to Lutheran General in Trout Creek."

"I'll meet you at the hospital, Lillian. Take care."

As the vehicle pulled away, Harold turned to Eric. "This is crazy. Now we've had two break-ins the last few days. I can't remember anything like that happening here."

Eric asked, "I wonder if any food was taken."

"Food?"

"Yes. Remember the guy I almost caught. He'd stolen food from old Mrs. Thompson."

"I guess I'll have to check. I'd hate to think someone pushed Lillian down the stairs because he was hungry."

Another police officer approached. "Are you Harold Gustafson, the homeowner?"

"Yes. What can you tell me?"

The officer related several upstairs rooms had been gone through. The housekeeper had managed to call 911. When the officer arrived, he found a suitcase lying on the sidewalk.

"A suitcase?" Harold asked.

"Yes. I moved it over near the front door."

Eric looked. "That's mine!"

The policeman asked a few more questions, then Harold said he was headed to the hospital.

Eric thanked him for his hospitality. "I'll give you a call when I get to Chicago. Please tell Lillian I'm thinking of her."

*****

Four hours later Eric unlocked the door to his apartment. Immediately the silence wrapped around him like a shroud. Eric's thoughts were filled with questions. How was Lillian?

Why had his suitcase ended up outside? How did Mr. Sundstrom's daughter's body get under that cabin?

It had been interesting to watch Maxie jump into action when her dog focused on the scent. He enjoyed the short time he had spent with her. How could that be? It wasn't right. Claire had only been gone less than a year. But the drinking. Their relationship had not been very pleasant for the last few years. But still. He shouldn't be thinking about Maxie. Poor Claire. She didn't deserve that. Claire's memories once again surrounded him. Suffocated him. He unpacked his bag. It seemed like he hadn't been gone at all.

He walked to a window. A thick fog bank had blown in from Lake Michigan. It looked like he was standing in the middle of a cloud. What to do? He picked up one of the diaries Lillian had given him and turned to page one.

Chapter 13

(Two Weeks Later)

"YOU'RE GOING TO be on your own for a few hours tonight, Buddy."

He stared at his mother across the kitchen table. "Are you going out with Jack again?"

She smiled. "Yes. I'll make you supper first. I bought you some of your favorite snacks. Just make sure you stay in the house with the door locked."

"How come I can't come with you guys like last time?"

Christine thought for a moment. "Because sometimes grownups like to spend time together. Every now and then, they like to be able to...to just..." She stood and set her empty cereal bowl in the sink. "Darn it, Buddy. Don't you go and start making me feel guilty. I'll be home around nine o'clock. I'm sure you can do without your mother for a few hours. Now finish up your breakfast. You don't want to be late for school."

Buddy grabbed his books and ran out the door.

Jack opened his car door and was about to get in when he noticed Buddy. "You want a ride to school?"

"Sure." Buddy paused. "Um, I better ask my mom."

Jack lit a cigarette. "Good idea."

A few minutes later Buddy got in the car. "She said okay. Where you going?"

Jack stared at him. "What do we have here? Some kind of FBI agent in training? Why do you need to know where I'm going?"

"Sorry. I just wish I was going someplace fun instead of school. I'm sick of being grounded. He smiled. "But I think I know where you're going."

Jack's expression changed. "Oh, yeah? Where's that?"

Buddy pointed to the binocular case that was strung over Jack's shoulder. "Bird watching."

Jack nodded. "Yep. Guess you must be in the junior FBI training program." A few minutes later, he pulled into the school parking lot. "Here you go. Not much of a ride. Only five blocks."

Buddy opened the door. "I wanted to come with you and Ma tonight, but she said no."

Jack reached over and ruffled his hair. "Next time. See you later."

Jack took Lake Shore Road to the main highway then turned right onto Summit Drive. He drove to Ledge Park and stopped the car. It was a ten-minute walk down Summit Trail to the spot where a large boulder rested next to a six hundred foot drop off.

Jack took the binoculars from the case and positioned himself against the rock. This placed him in a perfect position to gaze down at all of the cabins. He could see every car that drove in. He slipped a bottle of water from his pocket and set it down in the grass. He'd been coming to the park three times a week since he had arrived. Jack hoped Buddy hadn't forgotten the talk he had with him about what to say if anybody came looking for him.

After three hours, Jack stood. He stretched, picked up his water bottle, put the binoculars back in the case, and returned to his car. Nothing looked unusual. That was good.

*****

The next morning Buddy was lying on his bed when his mother walked in. "I have good news."

He tossed down his comic. "What?"

"I ran into Darrell's mother at the restaurant last night. She said you can go over and play with him again after school if you want to."

Buddy bounded off the bed. "Really? That's great."

Christine held up her hand. "No canoes."

At three-thirty, Buddy and Darrell walked back to Darrell's house. "I can't believe they found a body buried under your place," Darrell said. "Man, that's so cool."

"Cool? I don't know about that. It was kinda creepy. Last night I had a dream about sleeping over a dead guy that came alive and chased me all over the place. Move *your* bed over some kinda grave and see how you like it."

"Did you see it? Was it all gross and everything?"

"I didn't get to see anything. Once that lady with the dog thought she found something, they made us all go to the front."

They walked into Darrell's room. He asked, "What you want to do?"

"I dunno. Got any new comics?"

"I got a couple." Darrell spun around with a huge grin. "Oh, wait! You don't know."

"What don't I know?"

Darrell put his fingers to his lips. "Shhh. Come on. Let's go outside."

Buddy followed his friend out the back door. They sat down on a bench next to an apple tree.

"I couldn't tell you about the tree house with Mom around. She'd go nuts if she found out I'm still sneaking over there."

"Have you worked on it?"

"That's what I wanted to tell you. It's almost done, and it looks crazy. It's got a real roof. A couple of windows. Two big rooms. It's almost like a real house."

"Sure, it does. What other nutty stories are you going to tell me?"

"I'm not kidding."

"You know how to do all that stuff?" Buddy reached up and grabbed an apple. "I don't think so."

"No, dummy. I didn't do it. The hermit did."

Buddy took a bite and made a face. "Ugg, this apple's sour." He spit the piece onto the ground. "Darrell, what's with you? You think I'm stupid enough to believe that old hermit took time to build our tree house?"

Darrell jumped up. "He did. I snuck over there a few days after we found that bone. I used Chuck's canoe again. When I got there, I was trying to put up another wall on the treehouse, but I couldn't do it cause it was too heavy. Somebody yelled at me. When I looked down, that hermit guy was there. He said he used to be a carpenter and he'd build the tree house if I brought him tools and food every couple of days."

"Where'd you get the food?"

Darrell smiled. "I snuck it from our house and some from my Grandma. I bought some baloney and bread too."

"The tree house is almost done?"

"Yeah. You won't believe how great it is." Darrell snapped his fingers. "I know. Let's go over there. I need to bring Paul some food, anyway."

"Paul?"

"That's the hermit's name."

Buddy thought about what his mother said. "I can't go."

"Why?"

103

"Ma doesn't want me messing around with canoes anymore."

Darrell punched him on the arm. "Come on. One quick trip. I got two chairs in the tree house now. We can sit up there and look all over the island. It's so neat."

"No. I don't think so."

"Okay. Too bad, after all the work you did finding those boards and straightening all those nails."

Buddy kicked an acorn across the sidewalk. "Well. Maybe. But just once. One quick trip. I really want to see it."

Darrell slapped him on the back. "Good. Give me a minute to sneak out some more food from the kitchen. You wait here."

Half an hour later, they launched the borrowed canoe and were paddling toward the island. It was a crisp fall day. Buddy sat in the front. Every few minutes, the wind blew a cold spray of water onto his left side. He glanced up at the sky. "Look. There goes a bunch of geese."

Darrell watched as the long V of birds flew overhead. He dipped his paddle into the water and pulled. "This wind's hard to work against. I'm trying to steer toward the tree house, but we aren't getting anywhere near where we usually land."

Buddy turned. "I wondered what was going on. It seems like the current's a lot stronger too."

"You gotta paddle faster," Darrell yelled. "Were gonna miss the island altogether."

"What's going on? Maybe we should turn around," Buddy yelled back.

"We can't. If we get sideways in this wind, we'll tip over. We need to move ourselves off the seats. Get lower. Get onto your knees on the bottom, but be —"

As Buddy tried to slide off the seat, he leaned a little too far to the right.

"Buddy! Stop!"

A gust of wind caught them, and the canoe flipped over. Both boys splashed into the cold water. "Grab onto the boat!" Darrell cried out.

Buddy let go of the paddle and flailed around in the choppy water. Finally, he was able to reach the canoe, which was now upside down.

"Help! Help!" Darrell called out.

"I'm freezing,"

"I know. We gotta get outta here somehow."

Chapter 14

PAUL SYKES WAS heating up a can of beans on the small wood stove when he heard screams for help in the water. He had propped open the door to let some of the smoke out from the dilapidated chimney. He hurried out the door and scanned the water. Something was bobbing out there. What was it?

"Help!"

Two small figures were hanging onto an overturned canoe. Was it those damn kids? He ran to the rowboat that was beached behind the shack and shoved it into the water. Rowing as hard as he could, it took him about ten minutes to reach them. "Hang on, you guys. Watch out. You're going to have to climb in here one at a time. Don't be too much in a hurry. We don't want this old bucket to tip over." He reached out and grabbed Buddy by the collar. "Take the side and pull yourself over."

Buddy threw himself into the boat. "Th…th…thanks." His teeth were chattering.

Paul maneuvered the rowboat closer to Darrell. "Okay, champ. You're next." He held out his hand and helped him into the boat.

Darrell flipped over the side and landed next to Buddy. "Can you get the canoe? It's not mine. My sister will have a bird if I lose it."

Paul watched as the canoe bobbed in the water upside down. "I don't see any ropes tied to it. There's no way we could hold on to it. Even if we could, with all that water in it, we'd never make it back to the island. As it is, this damn wind's pushing us out into the lake. I need to get us back to shore now."

Paul grabbed the oars and swung the boat toward the island.

Half an hour later, the boys were stripped down to their underwear and huddled next to the stove. Paul draped them in an old army blanket he he'd pulled off his bed. Their wet clothes were hung on the backs of two chairs next to the stove.

"Hope you like beans because it looks like you're going to be spending the night here. No way am I taking that rowboat out again. That wind's coming directly from the north. No telling how cold it's going to get tonight." He shook his head. "I'm afraid it's going to be a long night for your folks, not knowing where you are."

*****

Christine put the phone down and slumped onto a kitchen chair. It was after six o'clock and Buddy wasn't home. Darrell's mother was worried too. Maybe Jack knew where he was.

She walked up onto his porch and knocked. The wind was blowing hard off the lake. The temperature must have dropped at least ten degrees since morning. When he came to the door, she asked, "Sorry to bother you, but have you seen Buddy today?"

"I saw him this morning around ten. Why?"

"He knows we always eat around five. Here it is six-thirty, and he's not home. It's not like him to ever be this late."

Jack pushed open the door. "Come in."

As she entered the cabin, he said, "He's probably playing with one of his friends and they lost track of time. It happened to me all the time when I was a kid. You want a beer or something?"

"No." She glanced out the window. "It's getting dark. I need to get home, close to the phone in case he calls."

"Okay. Let me know if there's anything I can do."

The phone was ringing as Christine neared the cabin. She ran to the kitchen and grabbed the receiver. "Hello?"

Her heart sank as Darrell's mother told her that she just heard her daughter mention that her boyfriend's canoe was missing. Christine gripped the receiver. That damn island. What was it about that place that Buddy couldn't stay away from? She put down the phone. What should she do? Call the Coast Guard? Maybe Jack would have an idea.

Christine ran back to his place and pounded on the door. She shivered as she waited for him to answer.

Jack was holding a beer when the door swung open. "What is it? Is he home?"

She explained the phone call.

He walked to the window and stared out over the lake. "That's not good. If they took a canoe out there after school, maybe they're stuck on the island. That wind came up fast. I'm trying to remember what time it was. Maybe around three?"

"What should I do? Should I call the Coast Guard? Would they do anything?"

Jack continued to stare out over the lake. "We've got about half an hour more before the sun goes down. That should give me about an hour of light before it gets dark. I've been going fishing with a guy I met. He's got a boat in the marina. I know where the keys are. Let me give him a quick call and see if he'll let me take it out. I can make it over to the island in less than fifteen minutes." He picked up the phone.

Christine pressed her face closer to the window. "Would you do that? It looks pretty choppy out there."

Jack nodded and held up his hand. He talked for a minute and then hung up. "You wait here. I'll get a jacket and head out. Grab a beer for yourself from the fridge."

Ten minutes later he had started the eighteen-foot, twin engine Tiara and was headed out of the harbor. Even with the strong wind, the boat handled smoothly. It didn't take long to reach the island.

Jack steered the boat as close as he could toward the shore hoping not to see an overturned canoe. He spotted the tree house that Buddy had told him about. It was much larger and well-built than he had imagined. Did those kids put that together? It seemed impossible. It looked like something a trained carpenter would build. He slowed the boat down and scanned the shoreline. There was no sign of the kids. Maybe they'd made it to the other side somehow.

Jack pushed the throttle and the boat surged forward. As he rounded a bend, he noticed smoke coming from an old shack. He'd heard stories about a hermit that had lived there off and on, but he thought someone had told him the man died a while back. The light was fading rapidly.

As the boys were putting on their clothes, which had dried near the fire, Paul stepped toward the door and cocked his head. "I hear a boat."

They both ran over. Buddy pointed. "Look. There it is. It's going real slow. Do you think someone's looking for us?"

Paul stepped outside. "Could be. Come out here. Let them see you guys."

As the boys ran out, Darrell started waving his arms. He yelled, "Hey, are you looking for us?

The boat slowed and turned toward them. Buddy ran to the shoreline. "It's coming this way! They are looking for us. I wonder who it could be?"

Jack maneuvered as close to the shore as he could. He yelled, "Buddy, are you okay?"

"Yes. We're fine."

"Well, come on. Jump in. I need to get you guys back home before your parents go crazy." He looked over at Paul. "Who's this guy?"

Buddy said, "He's Paul. He jumped in a rowboat and saved us when our canoe tipped over."

Jack asked Paul, "What about you? You need anything?"

Paul hesitated. "Ah, I could use a little food, but I doubt you've got any onboard."

"You want to get off the island?"

Paul shook his head. "No. I'm good."

"Come and see me tomorrow. I'm staying at the Lakeside Cabins. Cabin number four. I'll get you some food."

Paul helped the boys onto the boat. "Okay. I'll do that."

Half an hour later, the boat was tied up at the marina. On the walk back to the cabin Buddy asked, "Maybe we could just stay at your place tonight. I think we're going to be in big trouble."

Jack smiled. "You got that right. What the hell is wrong with you guys? I know your mother told you to stay away from that island."

Buddy turned to Darrell. "It's all your fault. I told you I didn't want to go. You…you talked me into it."

Darrell frowned. "Oh, that's great. Blame me for everything. Some friend you are. Guess what? You can just forget about the tree house. I don't ever want you to play there anymore."

Jack said, "Now, now, boys. This isn't the time to fight each other. You need a unified front. And that's not really much of a valid threat, Darrell. After this adventure, I don't think Buddy's ever going to step foot on that damn island again."

As they neared the cabins, Christine came running down the sidewalk. She scooped Buddy up in her arms. "I'm going to give you a hug right now, but after that, I…I don't know what I'm going to do."

She let go of Buddy and gave Jack a quick embrace. "Thank you, thank you, *thank you*." She turned to Darrell. "We need to call your mother."

He gave her a weak smile. "Ah, you think maybe I could stay here tonight?"

Chapter 15

UNLIKE THE LAST trip he had made three weeks before, this time Eric was looking forward to returning to Red Cedar Cove. Harold had called him several times asking him to visit again. He said the old Victorian house was way too quiet with Lillian convalescing at her sister's.

Eric had continued to make progress on his latest novel but missed the morning breakfasts with Denton. He was looking forward to another critique meeting and was anxious to hear what they had to say about the next five pages he had selected for their review.

He pulled into the driveway, grabbed his suitcase from the back seat, and walked to the porch. As he reached for the doorbell, Harold appeared. "I've been expecting you. So glad you decided to come back. Let me tell you, with Lillian gone, this place is as quiet as a tomb. I'm going stark raving mad with nobody to talk to."

Eric stepped inside. "It's good to be back. I know what you mean about the silence. My condo's the same. Too quiet."

"Get settled upstairs. When you come down, I've got some cheese and sausage set out in the living room. I'll make us a drink."

When he entered Claire's old room, he was surprised again at how sparse it was. None of her clothes were strewn around like they always were after a few days into their previous visits. No empty drink glasses. He set his suitcase down and headed for the living room.

"Here." Harold handed him a whiskey on ice. "Brian's invited us to lunch again. I don't want to hear that you're not going."

Eric smiled. "Actually, I'd be happy to go."

Harold squinted. "Really? Well, that's good to hear. How's the book coming?"

"Very well. I added a new subplot after thinking about a few suggestions Denton mentioned. He's been an inspiration. I'm looking forward to seeing him tomorrow at the diner. You're more than welcome to join us."

Harold shook his head. "Not tomorrow. We need to be at Brian's place at one o'clock, so don't spend the whole morning gabbing with your friend." He started to say something but stopped.

"What?" Eric asked.

"There's something I've been wanting to ask you even though it's none of my business."

"This sounds interesting."

"Have you looked through Claire's diaries?"

Eric let out a deep sigh. "I have."

"Anything stand out? Or was it just a bunch of teenage angst?"

Eric smiled. "Sounds like you must have read them too. Yes, there was plenty of that, but the one thing that did surprise me was how close Claire was to Joyce Abrams."

Harold nodded. "They were close. For a while there, they were like sisters. It was very hard on Claire when she disappeared."

"Claire mentioned it to me a few times, but she never went into any detail."

"Probably too sad for her."

Eric stood and stretched. "The older I get, the more I don't look forward to that long drive from Chicago. I'm thinking about looking around here for a small house."

"That would be great. You, Brian, and I could have lunch together all the time."

Eric walked to the window. Denton, maybe. Not Brian. "That would be nice." He turned. "By the way, have you heard anything more about the body Maxie and her dog found?"

"No. But the rumor is the authorities are close to arresting Roy Sundstrom."

"Her father? Really? That's awful. How could a man do something like that?"

"He's a real piece of work. His wife left him. He can't keep help. Brian said when he worked there, Roy was always swearing at him and telling him what a terrible job he was doing. It got so bad he had to quit."

Eric sat back down. "I wonder what evidence they have. How do you put together a case based on something that happened so long ago?"

"I don't know. I guess finding Barbara's body under one of his cabins didn't help Roy's case any."

"No. That's not working in his favor." There was a long silence. "Did I tell you I got a card from Maxie a few days after I got back to Chicago?"

"No."

"She thanked me for the book I gave her. The one you found upstairs."

"That was nice of her."

"It was. I'm hoping to see her again sometime during this trip. Maybe she'll have some inside information about what's going on."

Harold stood. "You ready for a refill?"

Eric handed him his glass. "Sure. When's Lillian coming back?"

"Tomorrow. Good timing. She called this morning. I think she's getting tired of staying at her sister's. I asked her to come back since you were arriving today."

"I'm sure you miss her cooking. I've got an idea. How about I take you out to dinner tonight?"

Harold smiled. "That's a much better idea than trying to eat something I threw together."

*****

Paul Sykes approached the library and stopped. He stared at his reflection in the glass door. New clothes, new haircut, cleanly shaved. He smiled. The internet. What a crazy thing. Somebody had set up a fund for him after word got out of his heroic rescue of the two boys. It quickly grew to over nine thousand dollars.

He pushed the door open and walked up to the desk. "Is Mr. Lapeer around?"

A young girl pointed. "He's in his office down that hall. Do you have an appointment?"

Paul laughed. "Hardly." He stepped away before she could say anything. When he got to Lyle's door he paused. Should he knock? Hell, no. He pushed the door open and stepped inside.

Lyle looked up. "Can I help—"

"Don't you recognize me, Uncle Lyle? I look a little different from a few days ago when I was on TV all the time, don't I."

Lyle set down his pen. "It's amazing what a bath can do for a person. You should try it more often."

"Not a problem. I got me a real nice apartment. Free of charge for six months. Everybody in town thinks I'm a hero." He leaned closer. "Well, almost everybody."

115

Lyle pushed his chair back. "You did a good thing. Good for you. What do you want from me? A medal? Some kind of trophy?"

Paul pulled a chair over and sat down. "A medal? Sure, I'll take a medal. That'd be great." He slid out a pack of cigarettes and lit one. "I know. I shouldn't be smoking in here." He exhaled a cloud of smoke over the desk.

Lyle glared at him. "Look, I've got work to do. I'm not giving you another handout, if that's what you're after. I thought you were taking a bus somewhere?"

Paul planted his hands-on Lyle's desk. "Guess you thought wrong. I'm sure you heard about the body they found over at Lakeside Cabins, right?"

Lyle nodded.

"Everyone's pretty sure that's poor Barbara Sundstrom's body."

Lyle remained silent.

"So, my question is, twenty years ago when I came to you asking for help when I thought Barbara was pregnant with my kid, you said you'd take care of it. The next day Barbara was gone. She just disappeared. Never said goodbye, nothing. Not a damn word. Now they find her body over at Lakeside Cottages. I want to know what the hell happened to her. Is that how you took care of it?"

Lyle took off his glasses and spent a moment wiping them. "You can't possibly think that I had anything to do with that poor girl's death."

"I don't know what to think. All I know is, I tell you about my problem, you say you're going to take care of it, Barbara disappears in the middle of the night, and now…"

Lyle's neck turned crimson. "You're crazy. After we talked that night, I had her come over to the house. I explained to her

116

what a poor candidate for a father you'd be and asked her how I could help. She was terrified of that religious nut of a mother of hers. The poor girl was sobbing. I could only make out a few words. Mortal sin, out of wedlock, your name. In the end, I gave her a hundred dollars and drove her to the bus depot in Trout Creek. That's the last time I ever saw her."

"Oh, another bus ticket. Your standard answer for moving problems along."

"Excuse me. It wasn't my problem. It was yours."

"So how did she end up underneath that cabin?" Paul asked.

Lyle stood. "I have no idea. If you've got some hair-brained scheme trying to blackmail me for something I didn't do, you better reconsider. You may be the town hero today, but believe me, once the dust settles on this, you could find yourself in a very different position."

"Blackmail? Who the hell said anything about blackmail? I just want to find out what happened to Barbara. We had plans. I came to you when I needed help and look what happened."

"Maybe it's you who should be worried. If folks start remembering that you were her boyfriend way back then, I'm more than certain the hot spotlight's going to be shining on you. With that stellar carnie background of yours, I'm surprised they haven't hauled you in for questioning by now. If I were you, I'd take that money I gave you and high-tail it out of town as soon as you can."

"Leave? I got no reason to leave. You just want me out of the picture because I'm an embarrassment to the family. A stain on that fancy family tree you're so proud of. Leave? Not a chance. People have been nice to me when word got out how I saved those boys. Who knows? Maybe you'll come around someday too."

Lyle pointed to the door. "Don't hold your breath."

*****

It was a brisk forty-seven degrees when Eric stepped outside the next morning. The brilliant fall foliage looked like it couldn't get any brighter, but Harold told him it took two more weeks for the trees along Lake Michigan to reach their full potential.

Eric felt like a sponge as he tried to absorb as much of the surroundings as possible on his walk to the diner. The crispness in the air elevated his mood. It was nice to be back where the air was clean and noise pollution consisted of the sounds his feet made against a layer of recently fallen leaves.

He pushed open the door to the diner. The scent of pancakes and bacon enveloped him. Denton was in his familiar booth. Cheryl was pouring coffee for an older couple several tables away. She didn't see him as he slid onto the seat across from his other writing group partner.

"Glad to see you're back," Denton said. "I told Cheryl you'd be coming today, but it looks like you snuck right by her."

"I did. They're busy this morning."

"Leaf peepers."

Eric grabbed a menu. "What?"

"It's all the leaf peepers having breakfast. It happens every year at this time. Everyone wants to drive around the lake and see all the pretty leaves. If it were up to me, I'd make it some kind of law that they all had to stay home."

"Sounds like you've turned into an old curmudgeon since I've been gone."

Denton smiled. "No. Been one all my life. You just never saw him before."

Cheryl ran up to their table. "Mr. Ballard! When did you get back?"

"I got into town yesterday afternoon and just sat down a minute ago. I was going to say hello, but you seemed busy."

She pulled out her order pad. "It's been crazy around here for the last week. Lots of tourists driving around the lake looking at the fall colors. I'm so glad you're back. Denton and I met a couple of times at the library, but we missed you. I hope you can join us this week."

"I plan on it. I've been writing some new…"

Cheryl glanced up from her pad. "Oh!" Her gaze was suddenly riveted toward the front door.

"Is everything okay?" Denton asked.

Cheryl didn't hear him.

Eric said, "Cheryl, what's wrong?"

"It's…it's my…mother."

Both Eric and Denton turned toward the door where a blonde woman was standing near the register. She turned and was staring in their direction. After a few moments she walked up to their booth. "Cheryl? What are you doing here? I thought you were in college."

Cheryl's face flushed. "I…I guess I could ask you the same thing."

"I came here to clear up something."

Cheryl shoved her order pad back in her pocket. "What?"

"To tell the authorities that I'm very much alive, and that I'm not buried underneath a cabin like all the news stories are saying."

Cheryl stepped back and reached for a chair. "That…that was *you*?"

"No. Does it look like I'm dead?"

Cheryl and her mother stared at each other for a few moments in awkward silence. "Would you like to sit with us?" Denton asked.

Barbara didn't hear him. "What about your stepdad? Does he know you're here?"

"Dad? No. He knows I dropped out of school, but he thinks I'm staying with a girlfriend in Lansing."

Her mother clenched her fists. "What are *you* doing here?"

Cheryl looked around. "I can't really talk. I'm supposed to be working. But I'm trying to find out things about who I really am that you never wanted me to know." She glanced over at the woman behind the cash register. "I need to get back to work." She glanced back at the table. "These guys are helping me with my writing. Denton Morris and Eric Ballard. Why don't you sit with them? We can talk later."

As Cheryl stepped away, Barbara hesitated and then sat down next to Eric. She rested her elbows on the table and rubbed her temples. "This is all a bit much. It was crazy enough coming here to tell the cops it's not me buried under that cabin. I certainly wasn't expecting to run into my daughter who's supposed to be going to college." She grabbed a napkin. "I don't think she's going to be happy when she starts digging into things that probably should be left alone."

Denton sat back. "So, let me get this right. You're the missing Barbara Sundstrom. Well, won't Roy be happy to see you."

She glanced up. "That's not going to happen. I'm making a quick stop at the police station to let them know who I am, and that's it."

"But you've been gone for twenty years. I'm sure your father would like to see you."

Barbara stiffened. "I've…I've got to go." She slid out from the booth and quickly walked out of the diner.

"Now that's quite a surprise," Eric said. "Half the town thinks Roy killed his daughter. Won't they be in for a shock when they find out she's alive and well?"

"As will Roy. Can you imagine when he finds out that's not her under the cabin?"

Eric looked over at the door. "And that she didn't even stick around to say hello. I wonder what happened so long ago between those two."

Denton grabbed a napkin and wiped his forehead. "I don't know, but Roy's wife was something else. Very religious, in a wrong way. She looked down on everyone. Nobody met her high standards. She's probably the reason Barbara ran away."

Another waitress came by. "Can I take your order?"

Eric looked over at the cashier's area. "Where's Cheryl? Isn't this her booth?"

"She signed out. I'm taking over her stations. What can I get you?"

After they placed their orders, Eric asked, "Were you ever in the military?"

Denton raised his eyebrows. "Now that's a strange question. Yes. I enlisted in the Army right out of high school." He smiled. "Infantry."

"Where were you stationed?"

"The Philippines. Spent a lot of time in the jungles over there. Some covert op's stuff. That's when I started writing. I had to do something to keep my mind busy."

"Harold told me about what happened to you with your books. It sounds like you got a bad deal."

Denton waved his hand. "That was a long time ago. I guess I got published way too young. If I had waited a few more years, none of that would have ever happened." He smiled. "Bad

121

timing. Sometimes life's a bitch. At least there's one good thing going for me."

"What's that?"

"It wasn't my bones they found under the cabin or over on Winter Island."

*****

As Eric walked back to Harold's house, he thought about what Denton had said. How was it possible that he hadn't turned into a bitter, hateful person? A talented writer who was robbed of his rightful literary credentials because of the racism of the times. Denton's military background was impressive. He probably still knew how to handle himself.

Eric found Harold in the library surrounded by books and papers. "Looks like you're busy. I don't want to bother you, but something happened at the diner I think you'll find interesting."

"Really? Did Denton pick up the check again?"

Eric smiled. "No, it was my turn this morning. You won't believe this, but Cheryl's mother showed up."

Harold tapped a pencil on the table. "Okay. Um, maybe I'm missing something, but why did you think I'd find that interesting?"

Eric sat down across from him. "This may help. Her name's Barbara. Barbara Sundstrom."

Harold's eyes widened. "What? Roy's daughter showed up? She's not dead?"

"I guess not."

"What about that girl, that waitress that was over here. Why wouldn't she tell the police that the body they found wasn't her mother's?"

"Because she has no idea about her family history. That's the reason she's here. She's trying to find out who she actually is. Believe me, Cheryl was as surprised as we were, when her mother showed up."

Harold shook his head. "This story gets crazier by the day." He glanced at the clock. "Don't forget we're having lunch at Brian's house at one o'clock."

"I know."

Harold twirled the pencil. "I have to confess; I was expecting some push back when I told you about today's lunch. You didn't fight it. In fact, you seemed quite eager this time."

Eric grinned. "Miracles do happen. I'll let you get back to work. I have some reading to do upstairs. We're having another writer's group tonight at the library. I'll meet you in the foyer at quarter to one."

Three hours later as they neared Brian's house, Harold drove by the entrance to Ledge Park.

Eric noticed the sign. "I still want to take some of those trails. I'd forgotten about them."

"Talk to Brian. He knows them all. He can walk there right from his house. I think he hikes in the park almost every week until the snow flies." He turned the car onto Brian's narrow road and pulled up in front of the house.

Brian greeted them at the door. Once they had settled into the living room, Brian made everyone drinks.

Harold said, "You better sit down, Brian. Eric's got some news that's going to blow you away."

Brian turned to Eric. "What is it?"

"I was having breakfast in the diner a few hours ago, when who stepped in but Barbara Sundstrom. Alive as a person could be."

Brian's eyes narrowed. "That's impossible. How'd you know it was her?"

"Her daughter's a waitress there. She even had her mother sit down at our table. She was on her way to talk to the authorities to tell them they had it wrong."

"If that don't beat all. She just showed up out of nowhere after all these years? Well that's going to make the cops look like fools."

"So, who was buried there??" Eric asked.

Brian took a swig from his vodka tonic. "How the hell would I know? If the cops can't figure it out, I don't think I have much to offer. I tell you what, that Barbara was a very busy girl…"

"What do you mean?" Harold asked.

"You probably don't remember this because you were away at college, but Roy's daughter was keeping a whole lot of boys around here happy."

Harold smiled. "I've heard those stories."

Brian continued, "I know little Dickie Olson and Skip Jensen used to sneak over there all the time. She used to parade around like she was the Queen of Sheba when I worked there. She developed early, and she had no problem displaying her ample attractions."

"What about you?" Harold asked. "Did you ever sample the wares?"

Brian smiled. "I'm too much of a gentleman to answer a question like that."

"What about that other girl?" Eric asked. "When we were over at Winter Island, Harold said two girls had gone missing a year apart."

"Joyce Abrams? The doctor's daughter?" Brian asked. "What about her?

"Do you think maybe it's her under the cabin?" Eric asked.

Brian scoffed. "How would she ever end up there?"

"How would anyone?" Harold asked.

"You know what I mean," Brian said. "It wouldn't be too much of a shock if that body turned out to be some hooker or a runaway. Remember when everyone used to hitchhike back in the day. How dangerous was that? But Joyce? A doctor's daughter? Her family was right up there. Almost up with the Lapeer's. I think she must have run off somewhere."

Eric asked Brian, "Didn't you try to go out with her?"

"Me? Right. That's a good one. Too much diesel grease on me to be holding her hand." He glared. "Where'd you hear that? Claire?"

"Indirectly."

Brian set down his glass. "What does that mean?

"It's those diaries," Harold said. "I bet he found that in Claire's diaries."

Brian stood. "I'm going to set out lunch." He pointed at Eric. "God knows what your wife wrote about me in those damn things. She always gave me the cold shoulder. I'd take anything she said about me with a grain of salt if I was you."

"The ramblings of a love-lorn schoolgirl," Harold said. "I don't know how you can read that crap."

"Calm down, gentlemen. I don't remember saying anything about reading Claire's diaries."

When Brian disappeared into the kitchen, Harold pulled his chair closer. "I think you hit a nerve there."

"Apparently."

"Brian tried to get on the football team but didn't make it. We all thought he had the ability. He just wasn't in the right group. You know how high school can be. He and Joyce did go out a few times. I'm not sure how long they dated. Anyway, around that time she started dating Frank Mills. He was the football team's quarterback. That really pissed Brian off." He winked. "Maybe we should change the subject."

A few minutes later, Brian called out, "It's ready. Come and get it."

Brian spent most of the lunch talking to Harold. Whenever Eric tried to interject something, Brian made a point of asking Harold another question. After several attempts Eric stopped trying to be included in the conversation. Finally, Harold asked, "Brian, can you tell Eric about the trails at Ledge Park? He's interested in hiking there."

Brian shoved a forkful of potato salad into his mouth and chewed for a moment. "Sure. I walk there all the time. There's two trails that meander through a picnic area and a small camping spot. They're a little hilly. They cross a small creek and end up at a lookout over a big pond. My favorite is the Ledge Trail. Like its name says, it skirts the ledge. It's about six hundred feet high. In some places the trail goes right along the precipice. No fence or anything. You need to be careful. It can be slippery in the morning with the dew or right after a rainstorm. Every couple of years some bozo gets too close and falls over the cliff. You know how stupid people are these days taking those selfies. The views are outstanding."

"That sounds perfect. I'll have to make sure I take the time to get over there."

After lunch Brian said, "You know, I was thinking just because that body they found under the cabin wasn't Roy's daughter doesn't let him off the hook."

"Why not?" Eric asked.

"Plenty of reasons. First off, it's his property. Then, he's kind of a weird guy. When I worked there as a kid, I caught him peeping into the cabin windows a couple of times. For a while,

I'd say in the mid-eighties, he was letting some pretty rough characters stay there. Some motorcycle club from Chicago, if I remember right. They came by a couple of summers. When it finally dawned on him that they were scaring away his regular customers, he had to shag them off." He turned to Eric. "I'll bet you ten bucks the body under that cabin turns out to be some girl who ran away and ended up working for Roy."

Eric stood. "Which way to the bathroom?"

Brian pointed. "Down that hall and to the right."

"Thanks." As he walked down the hallway, he passed a bedroom. Stacks of clothes were laid out on the bed and an open suitcase was on the floor. When Eric returned, he asked, "Brian, are you planning a trip?"

A surprised look briefly crossed Brian's face. "Oh, the clothes on the bed? Yeah. Remember those concerts we were talking about the last time you were here? Well, there's going to be a reunion of a bunch of the bands I never got to see as a kid. I thought, why not. It's next week. I can't wait."

Harold looked at his watch. "Eric, I think we've imposed on Brian enough. Thanks for a great lunch. If I don't see you before you leave, enjoy the show. Call me when you get home and tell me all about it."

On the drive back, Harold asked, "What made you bring up Joyce's name?"

"Why not? You told me that two girls had gone missing. The one everybody thought was under the cabin turns out to be alive. That left the other one, Joyce. How would I know it was such a sore spot for Brian?"

"If you remember, they didn't disappear at the same time. I think Joyce went missing almost a year after Barbara. And then if you've been reading my sister's diaries, I'm sure she mentioned the bad blood between them. He always blamed Claire for poisoning Joyce against him."

Eric remained silent. Finally, he said, "It's always easier to blame others and never take the blame yourself."

*****

Jack was taking a nap when a knock at the front door woke him. He sat up, rubbed his eyes, and tried to work his way out of the fog. The knocking persisted. He pulled a small pistol from the nightstand, crept into the living room, and peered through a crack in the curtains. A man he didn't recognize was standing on the porch.

Jack snuck over to the back door and exited the cabin. He shoved the gun into his belt and pulled his shirttail out to conceal it. He quietly made his way to the front of the cabin and stepped up behind the stranger. "Can I help you?"

The man jumped. "Jeeze. You scared the shit out of me." He looked around. "Where'd you come from? Anyway, don't you remember? I'm the guy you said could come by and get some food. I rescued the two boys on the island."

Jack took a step back. How could that be? The man didn't look anything like how he remembered him. "Are you sure?"

Paul laughed. "It's amazing what a haircut, shave, and some new clothes can do."

Jack squinted. "Well, I'll be damned." He unlocked the door. "Come in. I wish I knew you were coming. I would have stocked up. Let's see. I've got some bread and cold meat. Would you like a can of corn?"

Paul held up his hand. "No. That's not why I'm here. I just wanted to stop by and thank you. That was real nice of you to offer me food. Let's just say, a lot can happen in a few days.

Some kind soul started a webpage for me. I've been able to move off the island, clean myself up, and stock up on plenty of food."

Jack motioned for him to sit down. "That's great. It was a brave thing you did. With that weather the other night, I'm afraid those boys were headed for a very bad ending. Thank God you were there for them."

"If I hadn't had the door propped open, I'd have never heard them yelling for help."

"You want a beer?"

"Sure."

Jack returned with two Budweiser's. "Here." He settled back into his chair. "Can I ask you how you ended up living on Winter Island?"

Paul took a long swig. "Let's just say I'm kind of a nomad. I'm a carpenter by trade. I've traveled with carnivals, circuses, shit like that. I hit some hard times a few months back in Florida, so I decided to come back here. I knew a guy who used to live over on the island years ago, so I thought I'd check it out. See if the place was still there."

"How was it?"

"Pretty damn bad. Took me a week to clear the rats out. Living alone on an island may seem pretty cool to some people, but it ain't. Starts to drive you nuts after a time."

"Were you there when they found the bone?"

"Yep. I was talking to that kid when his dog pulled it out of the sand. Damndest thing you ever seen."

*****

Denton and Cheryl were already sitting at a table when Eric arrived at the library. He sat down and pulled some papers from his briefcase. "Looks like you're all ready for the meeting. Am I late?"

Denton glanced at the wall clock. "You're one minute early."

Eric looked over at Cheryl. "I'm glad to see you're here tonight. I was hoping you'd show up. After the surprise you had today, I wasn't sure you'd make it."

"Surprise? I'd say it was more of a shock. I signed out of work early. I needed time to think. After a few hours, I called Mom and we met for dinner. I thought for sure she'd relent a little and tell me about my father, but no. She kept trying to get me to go back home with her. She said I'd only end up being disappointed if I kept digging into things that needed to be left alone."

Denton pulled his papers from a valise. "I'm just happy the body they found didn't turn out to be Roy's daughter. What a blow that would have been. At least you know something now. You know who your grandfather is. Maybe he can help you out."

"So, the mystery remains," Eric added. "If it wasn't Roy's daughter under the cabin, who do you think it was?"

Cheryl winced. "I'm not from around here. I have no idea."

Denton picked up a pencil. "I guess the logical conclusion would be Joyce Abrams. She's the only girl that's still missing. But for the life of me, it doesn't make sense. How could a doctor's daughter end up under that run-down cabin? She wasn't a wild girl, from what I heard. She was smart, privileged, and hung out with all the kids from the tree streets."

Cheryl smiled. "Watch out. I'm renting a room over on Trout Street."

Denton feigned horror. "Oh no! Keep away." He laughed. "I think the divide between the two areas of town was a lot worse back then. If you notice, there's a few not so elegant houses now in the tree area, and the fish streets have some very nice cottages people are fixing up."

Eric picked up his papers. "What do you say we get to it?"

An hour and a half later, just as they were finishing up, Lyle Lapeer came over to their table and said to Eric, "I'm glad to see you're back. How did the meeting go?"

"It's a rough crowd, Lyle," Denton said. "They beat me up pretty good tonight."

"Beat *you* up?" Cheryl laughed. She held up a stack of papers that were covered in notes. "Look what they did to me."

Lyle smiled. "I'd like to propose something to this illustrious group. I hope you'll be interested. I've been thinking about writing a book about my family. Even though I'm a trained librarian, I really don't know the first thing about how to construct a book. I was wondering if you'd like to come over to the house tomorrow evening for drinks. Say around seven-thirty. It would be a good opportunity for me to pick your brains about how you do it."

Eric glanced at Denton and Cheryl. "That sounds good to me. What do you guys think? Can you make it?"

They both said yes.

Lyle rubbed his hands together. "Wonderful. I'm at 624 South Elm Street. I'll see you tomorrow."

After Lyle left, Denton straightened his papers and said, "That's odd. Do you think he's really serious about writing a book, or was that just some excuse to have us over to his house?"

"What other reason would he have to want us to come over?" Cheryl asked.

"I'm with Denton. It seems a little coincidental that suddenly, Lyle's interested in writing a book." Eric stuffed his papers into his case. "But who knows? I'm sure we've all wanted to see what the inside of that big house up on the hill looks like. Now we've got our chance."

Cheryl grabbed her purse. "Oh, Eric, I hope you show up for breakfast tomorrow."

"I'll be there. Why?"

"Someone wants to see you."

"Who?"

She smiled. "You'll just have to wait and see."

*****

Harold set down his newspaper as Eric entered the living room. "There you are. I thought that meeting of yours would last all night. Come have a drink with me. I've been making Manhattans. My favorite drink when it starts to get cold."

"Manhattans? I don't think I've had one of those since Claire and I were here two Christmas's ago." Eric looked around. "Is Lillian back?"

"She is. She got here about an hour after you left for your meeting. She's happy to be back. I can tell you that."

"That's good. But with her arm in a cast, I'm worried I'll be creating more work for her."

Harold let out a laugh. "Are you kidding? She keeps telling me what a clean freak you are. How there's never anything for her to do in your room." He walked over to the bar and poured sweet vermouth into a cocktail shaker and added some whiskey.

"Even so, having another person here means she has to make twice as many meals."

Harold spilled some cherry juice onto the bar. "Don't worry about her. She'll be fine." He handed Eric a glass. "Here. Let's sit down."

When they were settled, Harold said, "Tonight for some reason, I've been thinking about my sister."

Eric took a sip of his drink. Where was this going? "You were?"

"Yes. I'm well aware of what a bitter woman she was turning into." He stared at Eric. "Let's face it, she was a drunk, and a mean one at that. I can't imagine how it was for you living with her toward the end."

"I can't deny it. Claire's drinking was getting worse."

"Tell me about it!"

"Harold, how do you know all of this? Who have you been talking to?"

Harold smiled. "You mean who was talking to us? Or at least to Lillian."

"Claire?"

Harold reached for the cherry that was bobbing in his drink. "Yes. You know how close Claire was to good old Lillian. Claire would call her at all hours of the night when she was blasted out of her mind."

Eric listened. How much had Claire told her?

"It upset her so badly, I finally told Lillian not to take her calls anymore. Then Lillian wanted me to talk to Claire. She knew you two were headed toward a separation. Lillian was very upset about how Claire was treating you. We both think the world of you. But I told Lillian there was nothing I could do. Claire never listened to me before. Why would she start now?"

Eric rubbed his forehead. How much had Claire said? Had she mentioned her affair? "The drinking was getting worse. I tried to talk her into getting some help, but the more I pushed, the more she drank. It was getting close to the breaking point and then—"

"I know it must have been rough. When I did take her calls, it was apparent she was turning into a stranger. A completely different person. A mean and vindictive woman. When did she find enough lucid times to write? I swear, I don't know how you handled it."

The conversation was giving Eric a headache. It was dredging up all the memories he'd been working so hard to forget. All the things he'd come to Red Cedar Cove to forget. He needed to change the subject. "I'm meeting Denton down at the diner tomorrow. Why don't you join us?"

Harold leaned against a pillow at the end of the couch. "After the drinks I've had tonight, I doubt I'll be getting up early. I'm going to leave a note for Lillian to make a brunch around eleven o'clock." He tried to straighten up. "I hope I don't forget."

Eric finished his drink. "On that note, I'm headed upstairs. I'll see you in the mor…well, whenever."

As he made his way along the upstairs hallway to his room, Eric wondered how much Claire had divulged. He entered the bedroom and got undressed. After talking with Harold, Eric's mind was restless. He turned on the nightstand lamp and reached for one of Claire's diaries.

Chapter 16

THE HOUSE WAS quiet the next morning when Eric left. He hadn't expected Harold to be up after last night's evening of drinking.

When he arrived at the diner, Eric was surprised to see Maxie sitting next to Denton. She noticed him at the door and waved. He walked over and sat across from them. "This is a surprise. Nice to see you again."

"I was just telling Denton how much I enjoyed your book. I could hardly put it down. I gave it to my dad. He's reading it now. I want to get one of Denton's books, but he said his are all out of print. I'm sure he has some stashed away someplace in his apartment."

Denton blew on his coffee. "Like I told you, my books were written for twelve-year-old boys. I don't think you'd enjoy them as much as Eric's."

"I'm surprised to see you here," Eric said. "Are you still working the case?"

She shook her head. "No. I've been off it for a while now. I moved back home over a week ago." She smiled. "That cabin was a little too much. Especially with what we found over there. Cheryl said you were back in town. I wanted to come by and thank you for the book."

"Do you live around here?" Eric asked.

"I'm about eighteen miles away. I have a little house in the middle of the woods. It does me good to venture out to civilization now and then when I'm not working." She took a sip from her cup. "Cheryl's been telling me about the writing group you have. She's very excited about it. It's so nice of you guys to take the time to do that for her."

"For her?" Denton said. "We're doing it for us. It's been very instructive for everyone. I'm especially interested in hearing what a younger person has to say about my writing."

"Me too," Eric added. "She's brought a totally different perspective to our group."

"Speaking of perspective," Maxie said. She leaned forward and lowered her voice. "This isn't ready for public consumption, but I learned this morning that they've positively identified the body we found under that cabin."

"It's Joyce Abrams, isn't it?" Eric asked.

Maxie nodded. "Yes. How did you know?"

"It was a guess, but not much of one. The town's had two girls disappear. One showed up very much alive a few days ago, so it wasn't a stretch to think the body we found would be the other missing person."

"Why did it take so long to identify her?" Denton asked.

Maxie pushed a long strand of hair behind her ear. "When it comes to these kinds of things, it really wasn't that long. It's not like you see on TV. Both of her parents were dead. They had to track down some relatives from her mother's side and do some DNA testing. They put a rush on the results. The testing came back last night." She glanced around. "Please don't say anything. I expect the news will be released tonight or sometime tomorrow."

Cheryl stepped in front of the table. "What's going on? Looks like you three are up to no good."

Eric laughed. "We're trying to figure out a way to sneak out without leaving a tip. Any suggestions?"

Cheryl rolled her eyes. "Yeah. I can tell you plenty of ways. Happens all the time." She set down a cup of coffee. "Here, Eric."

"Thank you."

She stood with her notepad ready. "Now don't forget about tonight at Mr. Lapeer's house. What's everyone having for breakfast?"

Cheryl took their orders and headed toward the kitchen.

"The Lapeer house?" Maxie asked. "What's that all about?"

Denton leaned back in the booth. "Well, I'll have you know our writing group has been invited over to the Lapeer mansion so we can share our writing secrets with Lyle."

"He's the librarian, right?" Maxie asked.

Denton nodded.

"I've never been able to understand why he'd go to work in that library every day when he must be sitting on a ton of money from the Lapeer fortune."

"I was wondering the same thing," Eric added.

"And I think I've got an answer for that," Denton said. "His father instilled in the kids that they had to make something of themselves. Lyle went away to college and majored in library science. His older brother studied economics and worked for a big firm out east. He passed away from cancer about ten years ago. That leaves his sister. She was the rebel of the family. She was the youngest. Spoiled rotten by her mother. She's been a wild child her whole life. Rumor has it she was written out of the will a long time ago."

Maxie reached for a napkin. "I don't know. If I had all that money, I'm not sure I'd be going to work every day."

"What would you do?" Eric asked her

She thought for a moment. "Probably travel around the world. Then come back and start a big animal rescue place around here."

Eric nodded. "That sounds rewarding." He looked over at Denton. "And you?"

Denton stared into his coffee cup. "I'd buy a publishing house and work with struggling authors."

"Great idea," Eric said.

"What about you?" Maxie asked.

"Hmm. What would I do?" He tapped his finger against the side of his cup. "Maybe I'd hire a few private detectives to try and figure out who killed my wife."

Denton nodded. "Then you could send them over here and they could figure out who killed poor Joyce Abrams."

Eric smiled. "I have my own theory about that."

Both Denton and Maxie stared at him.

"You do?" Denton asked.

"Who is it?" Maxie questioned.

Eric shook his head. "I can't say anything. It's way too early to speculate. I should have never said anything."

*****

Buddy ran up on Jack's porch and pounded on the door. "Jack! Jack! Can you help us?"

Jack opened the door. "What's all the racket?"

"Roy's over at our place. He's drunk and hitting my mother."

"What?"

"Can you help?"

Without answering, Jack raced over to the cabin. He pushed the door open. Roy was standing in the kitchen. He had a tight grip on Christine's arm. "To hell you're not. This is the third time I've asked you to come with me over to Trout Creek. I'm sick of your stupid excuses."

Jack grabbed him by the shoulders and pulled him away. He smelled alcohol on Roy's breath.

"Get out of here, Roy. You're drunk."

Roy stumbled backwards and tried to hold on to the refrigerator. He blinked a few times. "This is none of your business. I'm asking the little lady out."

Jack grabbed him again. "No, you're not. You're leaving." He pushed Roy toward the front door.

"Let go of me." Roy looked behind him. "You're outta here. All of you. Pack up your shit and get the hell off my property."

"Not a problem," Jack replied. "But first I'm taking you home where you can sober up. Tomorrow, if you still want us out, we'll leave. But you have to sleep this off first."

Roy mumbled something as Jack pushed him out the front door.

Buddy turned. "Are you okay, Mom?"

Christine rubbed her arm. "I'm fine. Let that be a lesson to you, Buddy. Look what drinking can do to a person."

"Are we really going to be kicked out of here?"

His mother ran her hands under cold water and splashed some on her face. "I don't know. Maybe. Even if we aren't, we have to be out of here soon anyway. These cabins close down in a few weeks."

"Where we gonna go?"

"I don't know. I've been looking for another place, but…it's not easy."

She pulled out a chair and sat down.

Buddy could see his mother was on the verge of tears. As he was trying to think of something to say, the door opened. He jumped. Jack stepped in and walked over to his mother. "Are you okay?"

She glanced down at her red wrist. "Yes. I don't know what got into him. The minute he came in, I knew he was drunk. He was demanding I go over to some bar in Trout Creek with him.

I kept telling him no. That's when he grabbed me." She turned to Buddy. "Thank you for getting Jack."

Jack stared at her raw wrist. "Are you going to be okay?"

She nodded. "Yes. But now I guess I've got to find us another place to stay."

"I wouldn't worry about that," Jack said. "I'm going to have a talk with Roy tomorrow about what just happened. Believe me, he won't be tossing anybody out of these cabins until the end of the month."

"The end of the month's only two weeks away."

Jack took a seat. "I know. I've been looking around too"

"Me too. I can't find anything I can afford."

"I've got a few irons in the fire."

She glanced over at him. "Good for you. I wish I did."

Chapter 17

DENTON WAS ALREADY at the corner of Oak Street and Lake Shore Road when Eric walked up. Denton said, "I'm glad we decided to walk over to Lyle's place tonight. It's such a perfect fall evening."

Eric rubbed his hands together. "It's a little chilly, but I like it. Why get in the car to only drive four blocks?"

They walked together in silence. Finally, Denton said, "I've spent the whole afternoon thinking about what you said over at the diner."

"About me having an idea of who killed Joyce?"

"Yes."

"I should never have said anything. It was stupid of me to open up my mouth like that. I don't know what possessed me to say it."

"But you must have some idea, or you never would have mentioned it."

"I may be jumping to a very wrong conclusion. It's too early to tell. But I do have a question for you."

Denton glanced up as the streetlights flickered on. "What is it?"

"You mentioned that you'd been in the service."

"Yes."

"So at one time you knew how to use a weapon."

Denton stopped. "Wait a minute. Just where is this conversation going?'"

"I'm just wondering if you're still proficient with a firearm or not."

"Eric, just what the hell have you learned? Are you in danger?"

Eric's jaw tightened. "Not yet. At least I don't think so. But I have a feeling that may all change the more I start poking around. I may need to borrow a weapon. Do you have a gun?"

"Yes. I have a six-shot revolver and a deer rifle. I stopped hunting about ten years ago, but every now and then I go out to a friend's house and we do a little target practice."

"I seriously doubt anything will come of this, but I just need to know what my options are." Eric pointed. "There's Cheryl. I'm glad she waited like I asked her. This could get very interesting."

As they walked up the stone steps to the Lapeer mansion, Cheryl said, "I'm a little nervous. I don't know if I should say anything or not."

"Say anything about what?" Denton asked.

"I wouldn't," Eric replied. "Just let the conversation flow naturally."

"Say anything about what?" Denton asked again.

Cheryl shook her head. "Nothing."

Denton stopped in front of the door. "Wait just a damn minute." He looked at Eric. "You've been talking in riddles all the way over here." He turned to Cheryl. "Now you just said something that I have no idea what you're talking about. What's going on —?"

A light flipped on inside the house and lit up a beautiful stained glass window. Then a bright porch light illuminated them. A huge front door opened. Lyle stood there smiling. "Come in. Come in. Oh, you're all together and punctual too. Very good."

As they filed into the foyer, Lyle held out his hands. "Let me take your jackets." He hung them on a coat rack, then pointed. "This way."

They followed him along a marble hallway. Denton glanced down at the polished floor. "Do you have a maid?"

"I have a woman who comes every Wednesday to straighten up. Mrs. Clermont. Do you know her?"

Denton nodded. "Yes. She lives over on Walleye Street, doesn't she?"

"Yes. She does a wonderful job." He turned to Eric. "I'm like you. I like to keep a tidy place."

Cheryl stopped in front of a large oil painting. "I saw a picture like this at the Chicago Museum of Art. Our class went there on a field trip."

"It's painted in the style of Monet. It came from France, but unfortunately, it's not a Monet." Lyle turned left down another corridor. "Here we are. The music room."

The room was round with highly polished wood paneling covering the walls. Heavy drapes hung from behind a grand piano. A harp sat next to it. Several Queen Anne chairs surrounded a thick table that held a pitcher of mimosas and a plate of finger sandwiches. Small sparkles of light from a crystal chandelier reflected around the room.

"Sit. Please sit," Lyle said, his hands fluttering.

As everyone took their place, Denton glanced over at the piano and harp. "Do you play?"

"I used to. My parents insisted on lessons for all of us when we were children. I hated practicing then, but now I'm grateful they made us. I can still play some tunes on the piano. I'm afraid my fingers would be shredded if I attempted the harp again."

Cheryl's head turned in every direction. Her eyes were wide, her mouth half open.

"My grandfather designed the place with the music room in the center of the house. He was quite the patron of the arts. He thought that art and education kept the populous civilized." He pointed. "A magnificent library is located through those doors."

Denton gazed at the intricately carved crown molding. "This room's spectacular."

Lyle poured everyone a drink. "So, as I mentioned, I was thinking about writing a book about my family, but unfortunately, I don't know how to start. I have all of this research I've done over the years, but I have no idea how to put it together. I'm sure you all do research before starting one of your endeavors. How do you compile it into a book? Where do you start?"

Denton smiled. "They do research totally different now compared to when I was writing. I used to use a microfiche reader and a catalog of magazine articles. Very time consuming. Everything's online now."

Lyle turned to Cheryl. "What about you?"

She squirmed in her chair. "Me? Um, I'm only writing short stories. I…I really don't do much research. I just kind of make them up as I go."

Lyle smiled. His gaze turned to Eric. "What about you and Claire?"

"We both used the internet a lot. It's so much faster than anything else. Over time I've built up a collection of books on crime procedure. She never used them. Said they were way too technical for her."

"What about her last book?" Lyle asked. "Did she do any research into the people or history of Red Cedar Cove? It seems like some of it hits close to home."

Eric reached for his glass. "Funny you would ask that. Harold said he saw elements of Red Cedar Cove in her book too. I read Claire's first draft and all the other rewrites of her manuscript. I didn't notice any of that. I saw her outline as she was working on it. The book isn't based on any particular place or people."

"But the part of the missing boy. And the big house on the hill. Are you sure some of those references weren't from here?"

Eric shook his head. "Not that I know of. If that's what she was putting into her book, she never mentioned it to me."

"What about your book, Lyle?" Denton asked. "How far back do you want to go?"

"I have records that go back to the court of Louis the Fifteenth in seventeen seventy-three."

"Your relatives are from the court of Louis the Fifteenth?" Cheryl asked.

"One of them was." He paused. "Well, she was actually a courtesan for the king, so I guess you could say she was part of the court." Lyle grinned. "How much closer can you get?"

"How much information do you have?" Denton asked.

"A lot. My study's crammed with books, copies of records, old pictures. You name it. I've spent the last thirty years collecting. It would take a lot of work to go through everything and put it into something that made sense." He looked around the room. "Any takers?"

Eric said, "Lyle, I don't think anyone here is qualified for a job like that, and I'm not putting anyone down. You need someone who's familiar with how to write a memoir. A very extensive memoir. I'm afraid none of us have that background."

Lyle picked up a sandwich. "Oh, come on. Writing's writing, isn't it? Like Hemingway said, 'you just sit down at the typewriter and bleed.'"

"Just so I'm clear on this," Denton asked. "You don't really want to learn about how to write, you're more interested in finding someone to go through all of your material and put the book together."

Lyle nodded. "As of now, yes. When we first talked, I actually was considering learning what I could and then attempting it myself. But to get ready for this meeting, I went to my study and started poking around all the files I have. It didn't take me long to realize it was just way too much."

"I have some contacts at my publishing house in Chicago," Eric said. "I can ask around when I get back. But something on that scale wouldn't be cheap."

"And that's the problem," Lyle said. "I realize this is more of a vanity project than anything else. I doubt if the masses are just waiting around to read everything there is to know about my family." He sighed. "It's probably never going to happen. Now that I think about it, I can understand writing a fiction novel would be much different than writing a memoir."

Lyle moved on to the history of some of the paintings that lined the walls in the room. He explained where they came from in France, who painted them, and how his grandfather had everything transported to the states.

Eric sipped his drink. The mood had changed. It seemed like once Lyle understood they were not going to be able to help him, he was now wanting to quickly wrap things up.

Lyle stood. "Well, it was so wonderful of you all to come and pay me a visit. I've had such a good time. I hope to see you at your weekly writing group. I've learned so much about the craft that I didn't know before."

They followed him back through the long corridors, got their jackets, and stepped out into the darkness. As the heavy wooden door closed behind them, Denton said, "What an impressive house. I wish we could have seen more of it."

Eric shivered. "The wind's picked up. Feels like the temperature dropped about twenty degrees." He glanced over at Cheryl. "Are you okay?"

"No. I'm mad at myself. I wanted to say something, but I just couldn't think of a way to start. Now that our little meeting's over, I'm very disappointed."

Denton took a step down the marble stairs. "I'm not even going to ask. You people are full of all kinds of secrets."

"It's not a secret, Denton," Cheryl said. "Just some stupid idea I've got in my head." She followed him.

When they got to the corner, Eric said, "Would you like us to walk you to your place?"

She shook her head. "No. It's completely in the opposite direction. I'll be fine."

Cheryl turned left and continued for half a block. She glanced over her shoulder. Eric and Denton had disappeared into the gloom of the evening. She closed her eyes. She should have said something. But why make a scene in front of everybody? Now everyone was gone. Just Mr. Lapeer sitting in that huge house by himself. With his finger sandwiches. His fancy paintings. His....

She spun around. Should she do this? Now was as good a time as any. At least get it over with. She'd feel a lot better, one way or another.

Back at Lyle's house, she banged on the big wooden door. She waited a minute and then knocked again. Where was he? He couldn't have gone to bed that quickly. It seemed like forever before the porch light switched back on.

Lyle stuck his head out from behind the door. "Oh. It's you. Did you forget something?"

Cheryl stepped closer. "Forget something?" No, I didn't forget any—"

"Well, what is it then?"

"I'm…I'm that girl that called you. Remember? The girl that thought we could be related."

Lyle stared at her with a look of bewilderment, then his eyes widened. "That's it. For some reason I thought your voice sounded familiar. For the life of me, I couldn't place where I'd heard it before." He glared. "I thought I told you that you were wrong and to leave me alone."

"But I've done the DNA testing. The report showed I had relatives here in Red Cedar Cove. The Lapeers."

"That's impossible. I've never been married. I'm afraid this conversation is over." He started to close the door.

"But wait! My mother was just in town. You probably saw her on television."

Lyle paused. "On television?"

"Yes. My mother's Barbara Sundstrom. They thought she was dead, but…"

"What has this got to do with me? Nothing!" He slammed the door closed.

The porch light switched off surrounding her in darkness.

****

Eric heard loud talking when he entered the foyer of Harold's house. He glanced at his watch. It was a quarter to ten. The voices were coming from the living room. He heard Brian let out a loud laugh. "Those were the days. Remember the dances we used to go to in Trout Creek? What was the name of that band we liked?

"The Prophets. That's who they were. Remember, they all wore black."

Brian burst out laughing. "Just like Lillian!"

Eric glanced up the staircase. Should he just sneak upstairs? Maybe read some more of Claire's diaries? No. It wasn't even ten o'clock. How would he explain that to Harold the next morning? He sighed and headed toward the room.

"Well look what the cat dragged in," Brian bellowed. "I'm surprised you decided to come back here after hobnobbing with Lyle Lapeer."

Eric decided to play along. "I know. It was a hard decision. But after we went through all the champagne and caviar, I thought, what the hell."

Brian picked up a bottle of Maker's Mark bourbon and poured out a shot. "We don't have any champagne, but here, take this."

"Thanks."

"How was the fancy party?" Harold asked. "Was Lyle full of himself like usual?"

"It was nice. We saw a little of the house. It's quite the place."

Brian said, "Yeah. I was over there for tea and crumpets a few times."

Harold turned, "You were?"

Brian burst out laughing, spitting out some of his drink. "Right. That'd be the day I got invited over there. Lyle would be terrified I'd get diesel grease all over everything from my big fat ass."

Harold ignored him. "Eric, that dog lady called here for you too. She wants to meet you for lunch tomorrow. I took down her number. It's up on your nightstand."

Brian reached for the bourbon bottle. "Whoa! Moving kind of fast, aren't you?" He smiled. "I guess I can't blame you much. Harold tells me Claire was quite the bitch toward the end."

Harold spun around. "Brian!"

"What?" Eric asked staring at Harold.

"Now, Brian, I only said Claire's drinking had gotten out of hand." He stepped over and tried to take the shot glass. "I think you've had…"

Brian grabbed Harold's arm. "Not so fast". He downed the whiskey and pushed Harold away.

"Now wait a minute," Eric said. He stepped between them. "There's no need for that. Harold's right. Looks like you've had your share for tonight."

Brian pulled back and punched Eric in the face, sending him crashing into his brother-in-law. Harold stumbled, tried to catch his balance, and then fell against a floor lamp. It toppled over and hit the floor with a bang.

Eric felt his cheekbone. He didn't seem to be bleeding.

Harold jumped back to his feet. "Stop it. Eric's right. We've both had enough to drink for one night."

Brian turned. "Everything was great until he showed up. Remember who your friends are, Harold."

Eric grabbed Brian by the shoulder. "Come on. It's time for you to leave." He escorted him to the foyer and opened the door.

Brian grabbed his jacket from the coat rack and stepped onto the porch. "I'm glad you ended up with that bitch after all. Better you than me. Why don't you go back to Chicago where you belong?" He turned toward his car.

Eric closed the door and flipped the deadbolt. He stopped at the bathroom and stared in the mirror. His cheek was red and swollen. He ran cold water on a washcloth and patted his face.

When he returned, Harold had set the lamp back up. Shards of glass from a broken globe littered the floor.

Lillian appeared in the doorway wrapped in a robe. She surveyed the room. "What's going on down here?"

"Brian had a little too much to drink and became belligerent," Harold said.

"Again?" She looked at Eric. "Did he hit you?"

Eric reached for his face. "He did. He's pretty quick for a drunk. I never saw it coming."

Harold picked up the Maker's Mark bottle and put it away. "God, I'm so sorry, Eric. Brian was half in the bag when he got here. He just kept pouring them down."

"At least there's one good thing that came out of tonight," Eric said.

"What's that?"

"I'm done having lunch with your buddy. From now on, you're on your own."

"I'm sure he'll call here in the morning and apologize to you."

"What good is that going to do? He can save his breath. Harold, what do you see in that guy? He's a bitter, jealous man who drinks too much. I can't imagine you being friends with someone like that."

"We go back a long way. Let's leave it at that."

Lillian shook her head and left the room.

Eric looked down at the broken glass. "Can I help you with this?'

"No. It will only take a minute."

"All right, then. If I can't help, I'm going to go to bed."

"Goodnight."

When Eric got upstairs, he looked at his face again. The redness in the bruise was turning a slight purple. He put on his pajamas. As he was getting into bed, he noticed the diary he had been reading was on the floor. He picked it up. That's not where he had left it.

Chapter 18

ERIC WAS THE first one downstairs the next morning. He rummaged around the kitchen and was making eggs and bacon when Harold shuffled in. His hair was uncombed. He was in his bathrobe. "What are you doing? Lillian's back. You saw her last night."

"I know. I thought I'd make breakfast for everyone this morning."

Harold shook his head. "You're going to spoil her." He stepped closer and looked at Eric's face. "That's quite a bruise you've got there."

Eric gingerly felt his cheek "Too bad I didn't send him home with one of his own."

"Now, now, Eric. You're a better man than he is." Harold reached up and massaged his temples. "Damn. My head's killing me. Brian's a bad influence on me. He always makes me drink too much." He opened a cupboard and took down a glass. "I'm headed to the bathroom for an Alka-Seltzer. You want one?"

"No. I'm fine. You're down just in time. Breakfast will be ready in a few minutes."

"Where's Lillian?"

"I sent her back upstairs. I told her I was cooking this morning. I said I'd let her know when it was time to eat."

When Harold returned from the bathroom, his hair was combed. He looked a lot better. "No diner this morning?"

"Denton told me he wasn't going to make it. I didn't feel like sitting there by myself."

"Good. Looks like you've cooked up a great breakfast."

"Thanks. I hope you don't mind me rummaging around your pantry." He scooped eggs onto three plates and added strips of bacon. "Here. Grab a coffee. Toast is already out there. We're ready to eat. Let me get Lillian."

Just as Eric turned to get her, she walked in. "Goodness, it smells delicious." She glanced over at the stove. "And you didn't make a big mess like you know who does, when he decides to cook."

Harold held up his hands. "Now wait a minute. Have you ever seen an Italian chef cook? They use every pot in the kitchen."

"You're not Italian," she replied.

"Go take a seat in the dining room," Eric said. "I'll serve."

As they sat at the table, Harold asked, "How are you doing with Claire's diaries?"

Lillian glanced over at Eric.

Eric took a sip of coffee. "They're not easy to read. I keep thinking of what happened to her in Chicago. How innocent Claire was back then. They're filled with the usual teenaged ramblings. Does J like B? J asked me to spend the night at her house with L and M. Things like that."

"J? B? L? M? What are you talking about?"

"Claire used letters and initials a lot."

"Why would she do that?"

"Probably because it was her diary, and she thought it would provide some sort of anonymity in case you or her parents ever snooped around. I get the feeling that Joyce was much more outgoing than Claire during that time. Joyce seemed to be quite the flirt with the boys."

Harold munched on a piece of bacon. "I think you're right. Claire idolized her because Joyce was very confident and sure of herself. Claire tried to come off like that now and then, but down deep, I don't think she actually was that self-assured."

"Probably one of the reasons she drank too much," Eric added.

Harold nodded. "Courage in a bottle. You mentioned Brian. Did Claire talk about him a lot?"

Lillian glanced over at Eric again.

"She did. She knew he had a crush on her. But it sounds like he was making a play for Joyce too. That seemed to bother Claire, but it's hard to make out everything because of the code she kept using."

Harold scoffed. "Code? Like I was ever interested in reading that drivel. I was the older brother. Claire always said she felt invisible because I was always rushing here and there with my friends. She was my little sister. You know how that goes."

"I wish I did. I'm an only child. I was spoiled rotten. My parents were older when they had me. I always wanted a brother."

Harold picked up a napkin and wiped his mouth. "Well, you got me. Close enough."

Eric smiled. "Damn right."

"Hey, I have an idea. I've got to work on my manuscript today, and it looks like it's supposed to rain for the next few days. But after it clears up, maybe we can go hiking up at Ledge Park like you wanted to."

"Really?" Eric said. "I thought you weren't interested in hiking."

"It's more your thing than mine, but I want to take advantage of the beautiful fall weather we've had before this rain. We both know what's coming. A long winter."

"Sure. That would be great."

"What are your plans for this afternoon?"

"I'm going to call Maxie this morning and see if we can have lunch."

Harold wiped up the last of the egg yolk with his toast. "That's good. I think it's time you met someone nice."

Eric raised his hand. "Now hold on a minute. I'm not looking for romance. I just find Maxie interesting to talk to."

Lillian stood and tried to take Eric's empty plate.

He gently pushed her hand away. "No. I'm cleaning the kitchen. I made the mess; I'm cleaning it up. You relax, Lillian. I insist."

Harold pushed back his chair. "Interesting to talk to, eh? And if Maxie were eighty-two and full of wrinkles, I'm sure she'd be just as interesting, wouldn't she?"

Eric thought for a moment. "Well, maybe not quite."

*****

Eric stood in front of the Trout Creek Brewing Company for ten minutes before Maxie showed up. She looked different. As they entered the building, he asked, "Did you cut your hair or something?"

"I did. I can't believe you noticed."

"It looks nice."

As they settled into a booth, Maxie reached into her purse. "My dad handed me twenty dollars to give you."

"Twenty dollars? For what? Oh, I hope he doesn't think I want money for the book I gave you."

She shook her head. "No. He liked the book so much, he wants to buy the next one in the series."

Eric grinned. "Really? Forget about the money. I'll mail you a copy when I get home. I know Harold doesn't have a spare of that one lying around." He picked up a menu. "What's good here?"

Maxie smiled. "The beers."

"I like microbreweries. What's your favorite?"

"I usually get the Pale Fawn. It's a Pilsner."

"I'll give it a try. I like a Pilsner too. So many younger people are drinking those IPA's. They're too strong for me."

A waitress came by and took their drink order.

"Is there any more news about Joyce Abrams?" Eric asked.

She made a face. "My friend at the station told me the poor girl's skull was crushed."

"Is that what killed her?"

Maxie nodded. "That's what they think. Who could do something like that?" She grabbed Eric's hand. "Don't say anything. They don't want that out. He told me when they figured out the body wasn't Roy's daughter; it really shook everybody up."

"I can imagine. Everybody but Roy. Did you know I was in the diner when Barbara came in? She hadn't been to the authorities yet. Denton and I were shocked when we found out who she was."

"How did you know it was her? Did she make some kind of announcement in the diner or something?"

"No. Come to find out, she's our waitress's mother. It's a long story, but neither of them knew the other one was going to be there. Cheryl was shocked when she saw her mother come in."

Maxie thought for a moment. "So that means that the waitress, let me get this right, the pretty young girl that waits on us, is Roy Sundstrom's granddaughter?"

Eric nodded.

"Was she staying over at the cabins when we found the body? I don't remember seeing her there."

"No. She's renting a room over on Trout Street."

"Why wouldn't she stay with Roy?"

"Because as of two days ago, before her mother showed up, Cheryl had no idea she was related to Roy. That's why she came to Red Cedar Cove in the first place. To find out more about who she really is, and where her family came from."

The waitress came by and set down their beers. "Can I take your order?"

"I'm sorry," Eric said. "Can you give us a few more minutes? We've been talking."

As she walked away, Maxie asked, "So Cheryl's in town to find out things about her past, but she had no idea she was related to Roy Sundstrom from the cabins. What brought her to Red Cedar Cove to begin with? I mean, it's such a small community."

Eric sighed. "Something did, but Cheryl made me promise I wouldn't say anything about it."

Maxie sat back. "Not even to me? Haven't I been telling you things about the investigation that were supposed to be kept quiet?"

Eric nodded. "You have."

"Well?"

Eric picked up a menu. "Maybe it's time to order."

Maxie reached for hers. "Too bad. I had something else to tell you about the case, but not now."

Eric smiled. "You just made that up, didn't you?"

As Maxie was about to answer, his cell phone rang. He glanced at the number. It was the forensic accountant. "I'm sorry. I have to take this call. Shouldn't take too long." He slid out of the booth and stepped outside. "Hello Mr. Cohen. I'm fine. I was getting a little anxious. I thought I would have heard from you before." He listened. "Oh, interesting. What? Really? Are you sure about that? Yes, Red Cedar Cove? Not only am I familiar with it, I'm staying there right now. Well, I can't thank you enough." Eric put the phone back in his pocket. How could that be? It made no sense whatsoever. He paced back and forth. He needed to try and settle down before he went back into the restaurant.

When he returned to the booth, Maxie asked, "Is everything okay?"

"Well, let's just say that was an interesting call. Where were we?"

"I had just said there was something about the case I wasn't going to tell you."

Eric sighed. This wasn't turning out to be the fun time he had expected.

Chapter 19

Buddy was playing fetch with King when a battered green pickup pulled up in front of Jack's cabin. A man got out, walked up to the door and knocked. Buddy knew Jack wasn't home because his car was gone. Lately, he'd been leaving every morning and coming back in the middle of the afternoon.

The man leaned over and looked into the window. He knocked a few more times. As he returned to his car, he called out, "Hey, kid. You know the guy that lives here?"

Buddy almost said yes, but then remembered what Jack had told him to say if anyone came around asking about him. "Nope."

The man stepped closer. "Were do you live?"

Buddy pointed to their cabin.

The man looked over at where Buddy had indicated and then looked back at Jack's place. "Wait a minute. Are you telling me you don't know who the guy is that lives right next door to you?"

Buddy nodded. "Yep."

As the man took a step closer, King jumped between them and sat down. He stared at the man and let out a low growl.

"Is the man's name Jack? Jack McGill?"

Buddy shrugged his shoulders. "Don't know."

The man looked at King, stepped back, and squinted. "Is something wrong with you, kid? Are you a little slow or something?"

The door opened and Buddy's mother stepped out onto the porch. "Is there something I can help you with, mister?"

"Yeah. Nice to meet you. I was wondering if you knew…"

Buddy ran over to his mother. "She don't know nothing. Now stop bothering me or we're gonna call the cops." He tried to push her back into the cabin.

Christina looked down at Buddy. "What's going on here?"

Buddy whispered, "That man's trouble for Jack. Don't tell him nothing."

"I don't think you need to be asking my son any more questions." She turned, stepped back inside, and locked the door.

Outside an engine started. Christine peered through the curtains as the truck turned around and headed to the main road.

She glared at Buddy. "Okay. Now what was that all about?"

*****

Cheryl rang the bell outside the Lakeshore Cabin office and waited for someone to answer. The door opened; a rough looking man stood there. "You need a cabin?" He leaned closer. "How old are you? You gotta be eighteen to rent a place."

"I'm…I'm not interested in renting anything."

He turned and started to shut the door. "I don't contribute to no charities. Best you be moving on."

Cheryl stuck her foot in the doorway. "Wait. Please. My name's Cheryl. I…I think…no, I know…you're my grandfather."

Roy stopped. "Your grandfather? What makes you think that?"

"Because my mother was here yesterday to tell the police she wasn't dead. Her name's Barbara. Everyone thought that…"

"She's your mother?" Roy scratched the stubble on his chin.

"Yes. Like I said, my name's Cheryl. I work over at the diner."

Roy leaned closer and studied her face. "Shit. You look just like her." He swung the door open. "Come in."

Once inside, Roy pulled over a kitchen chair for her. "Sit down. You want some coffee?"

"No thank you."

He stepped to the refrigerator and pulled out a beer. "Me neither." He took a big swig. "Well, this is a surprise. I saw your mom on TV last night. I was hoping she'd come by and see me." He looked over at the door. "Is she coming?"

"I don't think so." Cheryl briefly explained why she was in Red Cedar Cove and how her mother refused to even mention where she came from or who her father was.

Roy ran his fingers through his hair. "So, you don't think Barbara's stopping by? Not even to say hello. Ain't that the damnedest thing? To think that I spent the last twenty years worried about her. Wondering where she was. Was she dead or alive? And she's right here in town but doesn't have the courtesy to spend ten minutes with her father." He shook his head. "I don't believe it."

"I'm sorry. I don't know what to say."

He looked up. "You don't have to be sorry. Ain't nothing to do with you. Your mother was a stubborn one. She wasn't afraid of nobody. Her mother was a holy roller. Spent a lot of time in church. None of that rubbed off on Barbara. That's for sure."

"Um, I was wondering, Mr. Sundstrom, would you be able to tell me who my father is?"

Roy took another drink from his bottle. "Mr. Sundstrom? Honey, you don't need to be calling me that. Call me Grandpa." As he stared at her, tears formed. "My goodness. Ain't you the pretty one? Just like your momma." He quickly took his hand and brushed his face. "Your father? Well, how do I explain that? I really couldn't tell you. Your mother grew up fast. And you know how the boys are. Seems like there were always a bunch of 'em hanging around. She'd have a boyfriend for a few weeks and then she'd change her mind and have another one. I really can't remember anybody in particular that stands out. Let's just say she was pretty popular around here."

"What about the Lapeers? Did they have any boys that were coming around?"

Roy sat back in his chair. "The Lapeers? Coming around here?" He let out a loud laugh. "Now wouldn't that be something. Hell no. They had two boys. Lyle and Stanley, but neither of them ever stepped foot around here." He laughed again. "What the hell made you mention the Lapeers?"

"I sent in for a DNA test and the results pointed to that family."

"Nope. I think they must have mixed up a few of the test results on you. You might try and get your money back. There ain't no Lapeer blood on this side of the family."

Cheryl stood. "I've got to get going. I start in half an hour. I'm on the late shift today."

Roy took her hand. "Will I see you again?"

"Sure. Like I said, I'm working over at the diner. It's real close."

Cheryl fought back tears as she headed to work. Maybe he was right. Maybe the DNA test was wrong. But why had it said she had relatives in Red Cedar Cove? Because she did. Just not the Lapeer family. She was happy she now knew about her grandfather. But what about her dad? How was it that her grandfather didn't know who it was that got his daughter pregnant? Did he really know but didn't want to say? Why would that be?

She entered the diner. The restaurant was almost full. Apparently the tourists were still coming around.

"Hey, Cheryl."

She looked over at Mrs. Smithfield, the owner. She was waving a small envelope. "This is for you."

"What is it?"

"I don't know. Some girl from the library came by looking for you. She asked if I could give this to you when you came in."

Cheryl took it, tore it open, and slowly read it. It was a note from Lyle. *Can you come to the library tonight at nine o'clock? There's something we need to discuss.*

Mrs. Smithfield looked at her. "Are you all right?"

Cheryl nodded. "I'm okay. Just a little surprised."

"What you got there? A note from your boyfriend?"

"No. An invitation to see Mr. Lapeer."

Mrs. Smithfield's eyes got big. "Well ain't you something!"

Cheryl read the note again.

*****

As Eric drove back to Red Cedar Cove, he wished he hadn't gone to lunch with Maxie. What had he been thinking? She had gotten a little defensive when he wouldn't share the details of why Cheryl was in town. But then there he was trying to find out more inside information about who the police were looking at now that Roy's daughter had shown up. He couldn't blame Maxie. Why had he agreed to meet her? Maybe it was just too early to try and connect with another woman. Who was he trying to fool? Claire hadn't even been gone a whole year. Yes, for the last few months the relationship had been just about nonexistent. Once he found out about the affair, his marriage had technically been over, at least emotionally. But then she won the Macintosh Award. That changed everything. They had decided to pretend to be a happy couple for a few more months, at least until the publicity of the award died down. The award meant prestige and money. Money that would be shared when they parted.

Eric's cell phone rang. Cheryl's voice came through his car radio. "Do you have a minute?"

"Yes. What's going on?"

"I was a little late getting to work. I stopped by and talked with Mr. Sundstrom."

"Oh? How did that go?"

"Ah, it was kinda weird, but that's not why I'm calling."

Eric slowed for a sharp curve in the road. "Okay."

"When I got to work, Mrs. Smithfield handed me a note."

"Okay."

"You're not going to believe this, but it was from Mr. Lapeer."

Eric waited for her to say more. Finally, he asked, "That's interesting. Do you want to tell me what it said?"

"Oh, I'm sorry. Yeah. That's why I'm calling. Forgive me, I'm a little confused. Anyway, it said he wants to meet with me at the library at nine o'clock tonight to talk about something."

Eric's fingers tightened against the steering wheel. "The library? When? At nine o'clock?" He thought for a moment. "I find that kind of odd. The library closes at eight-thirty. Why would he want to meet you so late? Did he say what he wanted to talk to you about?"

"No. He just said he had something to discuss."

"Have you decided to go?" He waited for an answer. "Cheryl, are you still there?"

"Oh. Sorry. Yes, I'm still here. I don't know. I guess I'll go."

"Do you want me to come with you?"

"Oh, no. That's not why I'm calling. I…I just was kinda surprised that he sent a note over to the diner, and that he wanted to meet with me. I wanted to know what you thought."

"Well, I agree with you. It does seem odd. Why would he want to meet so late, and what could be on his mind? You never said anything to him when we were over there for the meeting."

"Oh, wait a minute. You don't know."

"Don't know what?"

"I went back to his house after we left last night."

Eric took a quick breath. "You did? What happened?"

"I told him I was the girl who had called him before. He got mad and yelled at me to leave him alone. Then he slammed the door in my face."

"But now he wants to see you."

Cheryl answered softly. "Yes."

"I think I should come with you," Eric said.

"Don't be silly. Whatever Lyle has to discuss with me, I doubt he'd want to say with you standing next to me. That's really not why I called. I just wanted to hear what you thought about his note. Oh, wait a minute, Mrs. Smithfield's giving me a dirty look. I gotta get back to work." She hung up.

Why would Lyle suddenly want to talk to her? And why at such a strange hour? He slowed as three deer ate grass in a field next to the road. You could never tell what they'd do. They could be peacefully eating one second and jump out in front of your car the next. They were just as unpredictable as Lyle Lapeer.

It was four-thirty when Eric returned to the house. Everything was quiet. After a few minutes, he heard the floors creak as Lillian walked around upstairs in her room. Eric looked for Harold in the living room and library. He was nowhere to be found.

As Eric pushed open the door to his room, Lillian walked up behind him. "Harold's gone over to Brian's house. He didn't know when he'd be back. I'm going downstairs. I thought I'd put out some leftovers from last night. Are you hungry?"

"Actually, I'm not. I had a late lunch. You don't have to bother with anything for me. But thank you for asking." He looked at her cast. "How's your arm doing?"

She shrugged. "It's a bother, but the doctor tells me it's healing."

"Good."

She glanced down at the floor. "Can I ask you a favor?"

"Certainly. What is it?"

"Ah, please don't mention the diaries I gave you when Harold's around."

"Okay. But what's the problem?"

"Harold was furious with me when he found out I gave them to you. He's told me about it several times. I…I wish I hadn't done it, but I had no idea something like that would upset him so much."

"Well, Lillian, if this is bothering him, maybe I should just give them back. I don't want to be the reason he's upset with you."

She grabbed his arm. "No. You need to read them. Please. Don't stop. You have to—"

The front door opened downstairs. She let go of him, put her fingers to her lips, and then quietly returned to her room.

Eric went into his bedroom and sat on the bed. What was it with the diaries? All he had gleaned from them was that Brian had had a crush on Claire, and he'd been rude and obnoxious to Joyce and a few other of Claire's friends. He had a big mouth and a bad temper. Nothing Eric didn't already know without having to read her entries.

Eric glanced at the time. Ten to five. He had a few hours to kill before Lyle's meeting with Cheryl. He sat on the bed and reached for one of the diaries. It was nice to have some peace and quiet.

*****

Jack sat across from Christine. He cradled a cup of steaming coffee. Something definitely was up. He had never seen her so …what would be the word? Determined? He took a sip. "So what was it you wanted to talk about?"

She turned to Buddy. "Take the dog out for a walk. I'll tell you when you can come back inside."

"Aw, mom. Come on. I wanna—"

She stood and pointed to the dog's leash which was hanging from the back doorknob. "Buddy, I have to discuss something with Jack. Now go."

Jack sat back in his chair. Oh, shit. Something must have happened. What could it have been? He looked up. "What's on your mind?"

"A few hours ago, some man drove up and was asking Buddy about you. I could hear him from the bedroom. Buddy said he didn't know you. Didn't know you lived next door. He lied to the man. When I came out to see what was going on, Buddy ran over and almost pushed me back into the cabin. He whispered not to say anything about you because that man was trouble for you. That was the exact word he used. *Trouble*."

She reached for her coffee. Her hand was trembling. "So, my question to you is, how is it that my son knows all about this and I don't? I thought we were a…you know, after having…shit. You know what I mean." Tears formed in her eyes. "What have you been telling him? And I also want to know why you're living

167

here? Are you on the run from something? Are you putting me and my son in danger?" She slammed the cup back down. Coffee flew onto the table. "What's going on?"

"I'm sorry. You're right. I never should have involved Buddy in this. But don't worry. I'm going to take care of it."

"Take care of what?"

Jack stood. "I really can't get into all the particulars at this time. But I know what I have to do. It will get handled. That's all I can say right now." He turned to the door.

"Don't come over here anymore, Jack. And keep Buddy out of this. I don't want him talking to you or going near that cabin of yours. Do you understand?"

"I get it," Jack said. "But I'm going to—"

Christine pointed to the door. "Get out of here."

Chapter 20

ERIC WOKE WITH a start and glanced at the clock. It was eight-fifteen. He wanted to be at the library by eight-thirty. Eric hurried out of his room, stepped into the bathroom, splashed some water on his face, and went downstairs.

Harold called out from the living room, "There you are. I was wondering if you were going to stay upstairs the whole night."

"I fell asleep. I need to be over at the library in a few minutes."

"Didn't you just have one of those meetings a few days ago? Are you going to that group twice a week now?"

"No. Something's come up. I...I thought of something I want to look up for my book. They close in a short time. It shouldn't take me long."

Harold motioned toward the door. "Don't let me keep you. When you get back, I'll make us a drink." He smiled. "I promise I won't overindulge tonight."

*****

Eric slowed down his pace as he approached the library. He didn't want Lyle to know he was there. Entering by the front door would be tough. Would he be able to sneak in and hide between some of the narrow stacks of books? What about the back?

He walked up a grassy hill and approached the rear of the building. As he got closer, the back door flew open and a young man stepped out pushing a metal mop bucket on wheels. Eric slid behind a maple tree. The boy picked up the bucket and tossed its contents of gray sudsy water onto the grass. He walked back inside.

Eric waited a few minutes before approaching. As he turned the handle, the door swung open. Eric entered a narrow hallway. There was no sign of the mopper. He glanced at his watch. It was eight forty-five. Two doors were located on the left side of the narrow corridor. There was a sign on the first one that read *Janitor Closet*. The second door was open. Lyle was talking to someone. That had to be his office. "Have you finished the floors, Tommy?"

"Yes, Mr. Lapeer."

"What about the waste baskets?"

"Did them too."

"Good. You can leave now. I'll lock up tonight."

"Really?" the young man asked.

"Yes. I've got some business to attend to. I'll be here late tonight. Have a nice evening."

Eric pulled open the door and jumped inside. He waited long enough for the young man to leave Lyle's office. Eric pushed open the door a crack and glanced down the hallway. The library was empty.

Five minutes later, Lyle stepped out of his office. He turned off the main lights and stood facing the entryway with his hands behind his back. He rocked back and forth and stared out into the darkened entrance. What was that noise? Lyle was whistling some unrecognizable tune.

*****

Cheryl walked up the library steps and stopped in front of the door. The library looked dark. Had this been some kind of joke?

170

Suddenly the door swung open. Lyle motioned for her to come in. He didn't look very happy or excited to see her. She followed him down a narrow hallway and into his office. He pointed to a chair. As Lyle settled behind his desk, he said, "Do you have any idea why I asked you here tonight?"

"No."

Eric stepped out of the closet and moved closer to the open door.

"Really?" Lyle cocked his head and gave her a tight little smile. "How long have you been working with my nephew, Paul?"

"Who?" Cheryl asked.

"Come, come, my dear. We're not going to make any progress if you insist on playing dumb. You know, Paul Sykes."

"Lying to you? I've never heard the name Paul Sykes. I didn't even know you had a nephew. Even if you do, why would I be working with him? Working with him in what way?"

"Well, let's just say when I use the term nephew, I'm using it in a very broad sense. That illegitimate bastard child of my sister's is a far cry from someone who could rightfully be called a member of the Lapeer dynasty."

"I don't know what you're talking about. If that's why you asked me here, I may as well leave right now."

Eric moved closer to the closet as the sound of a chair scraping against a wooden floor came from the office.

"No. Please sit. It's not you I'm upset with." Lyle waited for her to sit back down. "Thank you. Now, say what you will, but I just want you to know who you're dealing with. Paul's a drifter who's never held a steady job his whole life. He associates with carnivals and circuses. That alone should tell you he can't be trusted."

"Mr. Lapeer, I don't know who you're talking about. Why do you think I'm working with him?"

"That's easy. He shows up out of the blue after five or six years asking for a handout. I tell him no. Then he shows up a few days later trying to blackmail me with some crazy story about a body they found under Roy Sundstrom's cabin. I tossed him out of my office. Then, a little while later, you come knocking on my door telling me that you're some long lost relative. I don't know where he found you, or how much money he promised you for playing this stupid little charade, but I can assure you he's nothing but a loser." Lyle stopped to catch his breath. "Where are you from? I know it's not here."

"What difference does it make where I'm from?"

"Because I feel sorry for you. Being suckered by that low life. I'd be willing to give you some money and buy you a bus ticket home. The more you're around that man, the more problems you're going to have."

There was a long silence, then Cheryl said, "Mr. Lapeer, please listen to me. I don't know your nephew, never met him, never talked to him. And I can prove it. When I came back to your house after our little writer's party, I told you why I was here in Red Cedar Cove. My DNA test kit said I was related to someone in your family. And if you remember, a few months ago I called you and told you the same thing. Do you really think that I've been working for months with this nephew of yours to dream up some hair brained scheme to...to do what? I have no idea what it is you think I'm trying to do here."

Lyle opened a desk drawer and pulled out a checkbook and pen. "Maybe you two have been scheming for months. I wouldn't put anything past him. How much will it take to get you to go home and leave me alone? How about five hundred?"

"What's wrong with you? I don't want your money, and I sure don't want a stupid bus ticket. Why would I leave now when I just found out who my grandfather is? I've finally made some progress in figuring out my past. I'm certainly not about to leave now."

Lyle put his pen down. "You found out who your grandfather is? Who is he?"

"His name's Roy Sundstrom. My mother came to town to tell the police that it wasn't her body they found under the cabin. That's when she told me."

Lyle's mouth dropped, and then he laughed. "Roy Sundstrom? Well that clinches it. If Roy Sundstrom's your grandfather, there's not a chance you have any Lapeer blood in you. Roy Sundstrom." He sat back in his chair and smiled. Suddenly the grin disappeared.

He leaned closer and squinted. "How old are you?"

"What? What are you talking about?"

"No. Please. Humor me. When were you born? You do know that, don't you?"

"Not that it's any of your business, but I'm 21."

Lyle's face darkened. "Now you listen to me. You're going to take this check and get the hell out of Red Cedar Cove. I don't ever want to see you around here again."

She stood. "You're a lunatic. I'm not going anywhere."

As she turned toward the door, Lyle sprang from behind the desk and grabbed her. "Listen to me, you little—"

Eric ran into the office and pushed Lyle off her. "Let go of her. She doesn't have to listen to you."

Lyle was sweating. He grabbed on to the back of his chair and tried to compose himself. "How did you get in here?" He glared at Cheryl. "Did he come with you?"

She shook her head. "No, but I'm glad he's here."

"Get out." Lyle pointed to the door. "Both of you."

"Not so fast," Eric said. "Now it's my turn to start asking questions."

Lyle stared at him and remained silent.

"Why was Claire sending you money every month?"

Lyle collapsed into his chair. "I don't know what you're talking about."

"Come on, Lyle. Man up. I know Claire was sending you five thousand dollars every month. It's too late to lie about it. I've got one of the best forensic accountants in the country looking into it. So, what's going on? I don't think Claire was donating to a charity. What did you have on her? Why were you blackmailing her?"

Lyle reached for the phone. "If you two don't leave the premises immediately, I'm calling the police."

Eric moved over to the chair Cheryl had been sitting in and sat down. "Good idea. They'll have a few questions of their own when they're done hearing mine."

Lyle put his head down and took in several long breaths. He slowly moved his arm over to the desk drawer where he had pulled out his check book.

Cheryl, who was still standing, screamed, "Eric, watch out! He's getting a gun."

Eric dove over the desk and knocked Lyle backwards in his chair. Lyle's head hit the wall with a dull thud. A gunshot rang out and a bullet lodged into the ceiling.

Eric twisted the gun from Lyle's hand and pointed it toward him. "Okay. Now sit back in your chair and answer my questions. Why the money?"

Lyle reached back and felt his head. Blood was on his fingertips. "You…you assaulted me."

Eric motioned to him with the gun. "It's the price you have to pay when you pull a gun on somebody. Come on, Lyle. It's time to talk. I already know why. Claire was having an affair and you wanted money to keep it out of the papers. How did you know?"

"How would I know your wife was having an affair?"

"It's not that hard to figure out. I'm sure I know the answer. I just want to hear it from you."

Lyle pulled out a handkerchief and dabbed his head. "You're out of your mind."

"It was at the National Librarian Convention in New Orleans, wasn't it?"

Lyle's head snapped up.

"That's where you saw them together, wasn't it?"

"I...I didn't go this year. I had—"

"Why are you lying, Lyle? I know you were there. Claire told me she ran into you."

Lyle sighed. "She did? Um, yes. I was there. All the top writers speak about their new releases there. I've gone every year for the last twelve years."

"So, stop lying. I already know about the affair. So, what happened?"

Lyle turned to Cheryl and then looked back at Eric and the gun. He bent his head down and stared at the top of his desk for several moments. Eric held his breath. If he was going to start talking, now was the time.

Slowly Lyle raised his head. His face looked tired. Tired and old. He wiped his brow with the bloody handkerchief and said in a soft voice, "One night halfway through the conference, I saw your wife talking with William Simons. I was excited just to be near him, he's won just about everything, and I was impressed that your wife knew him. Well, the more I watched, it became obvious that Claire knew him … um, quite well. I saw them together several other nights, and then I saw her coming out of his room one morning around three."

"So, you thought that would be a great opportunity to put the squeeze on her. She could pay you hush money to keep everything out of the tabloids."

Lyle's shoulders slumped. "It was wrong. I know. So wrong. But…the Lapeer money is dwindling down. I mean, with the stock market the way it is, some stupid investments, things are bad. I…I…thought—" His head shot up. "I'll give it all back. It's just sitting in the bank. Tomorrow I'll have a check for you. Forty thousand dollars. Yours. We can forget the whole thing."

Eric's eyes narrowed. "You killed her, didn't you?"

Lyle's mouth dropped open. "What? No. Why would you say that? I mean, if she was sending me money every month, why…why would I do something like that?"

"Maybe you wanted more? Five grand a month wasn't enough."

Lyle shook his head. "No. That's ridiculous. I…I was going to stop the payments. I felt bad."

"You were in our apartment, weren't you?"

Lyle squirmed in his chair. "Your apartment? No. Why would you say that?"

"Because you slipped up the night you had us all over to your house."

Lyle looked over at Cheryl like she had the answer. He turned back to Eric. "How did I slip up?"

"When Denton asked you if you had a maid, you said something to me about being a clean freak. How did you know I was a clean freak if you weren't in the apartment? You probably complimented Claire on how the place looked and she told you I was the one who kept everything nice and tidy."

Lyle removed his glasses, slumped over on his desk, and started to sob. "It...it was an accident. I was there. I came over to talk about her latest book. She let me in because she thought we were going to talk about the money."

"Why did you want to talk about the book?" Eric asked, still training the gun on him.

"Because I was mad about some of the things I had seen in it. It was clear she had put in things that would tarnish the Lapeer name. Our heritage. Things about my nephew." He glared at Cheryl. "I demanded she take them out."

"What did she say?"

"She said I was crazy. We argued. She slapped me across the face and then gave me a shove. She was drunk. I pushed her back and she fell. Fell right into a big curio. The glass shattered. A shard cut into her neck. Blood gushed out. I...I didn't know what to do. I panicked. I made it look like somebody broke in and I left." Tears ran down his face. "There was nothing I could do to save her."

Eric pointed to the phone. "Cheryl, call the police." He stepped closer to Lyle. "Lyle. There was nothing in that book about you, the Lapeer family, or your damn heritage."

Lyle pulled out a handkerchief and wiped his face. "How can you be so sure? You didn't write it. You're not even from here. Maybe if you were, you could see it."

"I'm not seeing it because it's not there. How do I know? Because I did write it. I wrote every word of that book. I did half the outline too. Claire was too drunk most of the time to be able to put together two sentences."

Lyle sat up. "You...you wrote the book?"

"Yes. I had to. She was running out of time on her contract. Everyone was anxious for her new one to come out because the book before it had done so well. I had to jump in and finish the outline and write all the drafts. I have no knowledge of your family secrets or your heritage. Let me assure you, whatever connections you saw in that book were completely from your imagination."

Cheryl turned. "You...you wrote the book?"

Chapter 21

THE NEXT MORNING Harold stood staring out the living room window. "I wasn't expecting this."

Eric walked up next to him. "Who are they?"

Harold pointed. "See that guy? He's a news anchor from Trout Creek. He's talking to his cameraman now. I have no idea who the other people are." He craned his neck. "Wait. Isn't that a Chicago station?"

"You've got to be kidding? All those people?"

"When you single-handedly take down the Lapeer dynasty and solve your wife's murder at the same time, I guess you need to expect some publicity."

Lillian appeared in the doorway dressed in her robe. "What's going on?"

Harold said, "Several news crews are staking out our house."

She looked out the window. "Whatever for?" She turned to Eric. "We were worried about you last night. I went to bed around eleven-thirty and you weren't home yet. Harold kept trying to call you."

"I know. Unfortunately, I wasn't able to answer my phone. The police were asking me endless questions."

"The police?" Lillian asked.

Harold turned from the window. "You'd better sit down, Lillian. Eric's got a lot to tell you."

As she took a seat, Eric pulled up a chair next to her. "Last night I confronted Lyle Lapeer about Claire's death and he confessed."

Lillian's hands flew up to her face. "Lyle Lapeer? No. This has to be a mistake. Why would he want to…harm Claire?"

James R. Nelson

"It's a long sordid story," Eric said. "He was blackmailing her, and he was upset about what he thought was in her new book."

"Blackmailing her?" Lillian asked. "Why would he do that? He's a Lapeer, for goodness sake."

Eric leaned back in his chair and let out a big sigh. "Apparently the Lapeer estate has been in a financial decline for several years. I really don't have all the details."

"But...how did you know it was Lyle? What even made you confront him in the first place?"

"Some things came to light after Claire's death. Financial things, and a statement he made when I went over to his house for that writers party."

Lillian wiped a tear from her face. "Poor Claire."

Harold asked Eric, "You don't want to talk to them, do you?"

Eric shook his head. "No. That's the last thing I want."

Harold walked over to the door. "That's what I thought. This is ridiculous. I'm going out there and tell them they need to get off my property."

"It won't do any good," Eric said.

"I'm sure you're right, but I can shoo them off my grass at least."

As he stepped outside, Lillian slipped a folded piece of paper into Eric's hand. "Here's some information about the codes Claire was using."

*****

Buddy's mother picked up his empty pancake plate and rinsed off the remaining butter and syrup. "What are your after-school plans today?"

"I don't have any. I want to go over to Darrel's house, but you won't let me."

"It's your own fault, Buddy. Every time you two are together, you decide to go over to that darned island. You remember what happened last time. Isn't there somebody else you can play with? What about the little park on Pine Street? Don't kids play there?"

"Them snooty kids aren't any fun. They used to laugh at Darrel and me. We hate that place. The only other kid around here's Tony, and you won't let me go near him."

"No, I won't. He's three years older than you. He smokes cigarettes and has a filthy mouth."

"I'm just going to play with that basketball you got me for my birthday. I forgot about it. I found it at the back of my closet. I pumped it up yesterday."

"Okay. I should be home around six. We're having sloppy joes for dinner."

*****

It was almost noon when Jack pulled out of the driveway for Trout Creek. He kept his eye out for the green truck as he drove into the parking lot of the Swedish Fish Shack restaurant. After a quick lunch, he headed over to where Paul Sykes had told him he was renovating a house.

The front door was open. He could see Paul busy taping new drywall. Jack yelled, "Looking good."

Paul jumped, then spun around. "Damn, you scared me. I've been working here since eight this morning and haven't talked to anyone. Take a look around. I've got to get this seam mudded."

Jack wandered through the house. It was a small two-bedroom place. He didn't know what it looked like before, but it seemed that Paul had fixed it up quite nicely. New kitchen cabinets, new floors. It looked like the only thing left to do was paint after the drywall job was finished.

He returned to where Paul was working. "Very nice. When do you think you can move in?"

Paul picked up a rag and wiped his hand. "I'm not moving here. I'm keeping my apartment. I'll be renting this out." He moved from one foot to another. "You know those cabins will be closing down at the end of the month. This would be a nice place for you. It'll be ready by then. Only thing left to do is paint the inside."

"I'm not sure I'll need a place two weeks from now."

Paul squinted. "What does that mean?"

Jack shook his head. "Nothing. There's some shit I need to take care of. Anyway, I don't want to waste anymore of your time. Why don't you stop by for a beer when you're finished here?"

Paul picked up his trowel. "I'll do that."

*****

Buddy grabbed his basketball and opened the front door. King bounded down the porch steps and chased after Buddy as he bounced the ball down the street past Jack's cabin. Buddy threw the ball over a low hanging birch tree limb. Why didn't they have a basketball hoop nailed up somewhere? There must have been other kids around at one time or another that played the game.

Buddy tried bouncing the ball under his left leg. He reached for the ball, lost his balance, and fell into the road. As he picked himself up, a green truck pulled up next to him.

A man jumped out of the passenger's side. "Hey, kid. My friend here tells me you know our pal, Jack McGill. Is he home?"

Buddy grabbed the ball and took a step back. He tried to see who was driving, but the truck was too tall. "Sorry. I don't know him." He turned and started quickly walking home.

The man took two long steps and grabbed him by the arm. "Don't be in such a hurry. We just need a little information about your pal, Jack."

As Buddy tried to pull away, King turned and started growling.

"Call your dog off, kid. I'd hate to have to hurt him."

Out of the corner of his eye, Buddy saw Jack's car pull into the travel park. The car hesitated for a second and then turned left instead of right. It disappeared behind the main office.

The man's hand was digging into Buddy's arm. He tried to pull away. "Let me go."

King stepped closer and growled again. His teeth were showing.

The man slipped a gun from his belt and pointed it at the dog. "I'm not kidding. Call him off, or I'm going to have to shoot him."

Jack ran from behind the truck, grabbed the man by the neck, and threw him to the ground. He jumped on top of him and tried to wrestle the gun away. "Buddy, grab the gun!"

As Buddy bent to get the weapon, the driver jumped out and ran over. It was the guy who had asked him all those questions the day before. As he reached over and grabbed Buddy's shirt collar, King sprang into action. He launched himself into the air and bit down onto the man's right wrist.

Buddy scooped up the gun and stepped back. "I got it, Jack."

King had let go of the man and was crouched down snarling in front of him. The man cradled his bloody arm and inched closer to where Jack was struggling with the other guy on the ground. As the driver pulled his foot back to kick Jack, a loud shotgun blast rang out.

Roy ran up holding a smoking shotgun. "You kick that guy, it'll be the last thing you do, mister. Get on the ground and spread your arms out."

As the man fell to his knees, he yelled, "Look at me. I need some help. That damn dog took a chunk outta me."

Roy looked over at Jack. "You okay?"

"Yeah."

"Help is on the way. I called the cops a few minutes ago."

The man Jack had tackled to the ground yelled, "You keep your mouth shut, Jack."

Jack stood and brushed dirt from his pants. "Too late for that bullshit, Johnny. I should have gone to the cops right after it happened. They're going to hear the whole damn story."

*****

Cheryl sat across the kitchen table from Roy. "I was surprised to see you in the diner this morning. You said to come by after I got out of work."

Roy took a swig from his half empty bottle. "You want a beer?"

"No, that's okay." She glanced around the kitchen. "Sure, why not?"

Roy grabbed one from the fridge, handed it to her, and sat back down. "It's been one hell of a day."

Cheryl untwisted the cap. "What happened?"

Roy related how he had to break up a fight with his shotgun a few hours before. "I got seventeen more days before I close this place up for the winter. I can't wait. Seems like the people staying here are getting seedier every year. Damn, I was thinking I'd try to keep this place open for two more years, but I don't know if I can take it."

"One of the men had a gun?"

"Yeah. Cops hauled them all outta here in handcuffs. I'm getting too old for that kind of shit."

Cheryl took a sip. "I don't think you asked me over here to tell me about something that hadn't even happened yet. Why did you want me to stop by?"

Roy leaned closer. "You hear about all that shit with Lyle Lapeer?"

"How he killed Eric's wife? Yes. Everybody's talking about it over at the diner. I was right there when he confessed."

Roy slammed his bottle down on the kitchen table. "What?"

Cheryl gave him a quick version of what had happened the night before.

"Well, when I heard about Lyle, that got me thinking about something you said when you came over before."

Cheryl's heart beat faster. "What?"

"You said something about your DNA test showed you had some Lapeer blood in you. I wondered who could that be? Well, I remembered something."

"You did?"

"Way back when, just before your mother took off, there was a guy hanging around here who kept bragging about being related to the Lapeer's. I didn't give it no mind because he was a pretty scruffy character. Didn't fit the Lapeer mold, and that's

185

putting it mildly. My wife kept trying to run him off. Said she didn't trust him with Barbara."

"Who was he?"

Roy scratched his head. "Went by the name of Paul. But I can't remember his last name. It wasn't Lapeer, that's for sure."

"What ever happened to him?"

Roy shrugged. "No clue." He smiled. "I've seen my share of transients around this place. They come and go. Only reason I remembered him was your mother was spending quite a bit of time with him right before she disappeared. My wife didn't like him, but then again, she didn't like anybody who was hanging around Barbara Ask your mom about him. I bet she'll remember."

Cheryl shook her head. "Wouldn't do me any good. She'd never tell me anything."

A car pulled in and slowly drove past the motel office. "Hold on a minute," Roy said. "I need to make sure I ain't got no more assholes stopping by McGill's place."

It was six-thirty by the time Paul pulled up in front of Jack's cabin. He walked up the porch steps and knocked on the door. Nobody answered. He knocked again. After waiting for a minute, he leaned over and peered through the living room window.

"Ain't nobody home, Mister. I suggest you get in your car and get the hell out of here."

Paul turned around to see an older man dressed in coveralls staring at him. He was holding a shot gun.

"Hey, what's with the gun? I'm only stopping by to have a beer with my friend, Jack." A pretty girl stood about twenty feet behind the old man.

Paul froze. Was that Barbara? No, it was the Barbara he remembered from so many years ago. How could that be?

The old man yelled, "Your friend's in jail. Got hauled off the property with a couple of his near-do-well friends. I suggest you do the same."

Paul walked down the porch steps. "Roy, is that you?"

Roy gestured with the barrel of the gun. "Don't try to sweet talk me. If you're a friend of Jack's, you need to get the hell outta here."

"Shit, Roy. Calm down. I only met the guy a few days ago when he came by in a boat and picked up those kids from Winter Island. You must have seen that story on TV. One of the kids' lives here. Buddy Nash. I'm Paul Sykes. I'm the guy that saved them. No need to be pointing a gun at me."

"The man who was living on the island?" Roy squinted and shaded his eyes. "You're a lying sack of shit. You don't look anything like that guy."

Paul laughed. "I got cleaned up. Come on, Roy. Put down the damned gun. You know me. I used to work for you a long time ago. Hell, you were a crabby old bastard then, I see nothing's changed."

Roy lowered the gun, turned to Cheryl, and nodded.

She stared at her father.

Chapter 22

ERIC FELT LIKE everyone was looking at him as he walked over to their booth at the diner. When he sat down, Denton said, "What's it feel like to be a celebrity?"

"What are you talking about?"

"You didn't see? Half the place was pointing at you and whispering when you walked in."

Eric quickly looked around. "There's only about ten people in here."

"And five of them were staring at you."

"Is that good or bad? Are they ready to kill me because they think I'm responsible for bringing down the lofted Lapeer dynasty?"

"Who knows? I'm sure just about everyone in town's still in shock. It's a hard thing to digest."

"Where's Cheryl?"

"She's not here. I asked the waitress that brought my coffee if she was working today and she said no. Said she was all excited about something and asked if she could have the day off."

"Really? I wonder what that could be."

The other waitress walked up to their table and set down a cup of coffee. "Denton said you'd be wanting this."

Eric looked up. "Thank you."

She took their orders and headed toward the kitchen.

Denton blew on his coffee. "Something wrong? You look a little distracted. Is it the Lyle thing?"

"No, well maybe. At least all those reporters weren't standing outside Harold's house this morning."

"So what's bothering you?"

"Yesterday I got a note from Harold's housekeeper that puzzled me."

"What did it say?"

"I don't want to go into detail, but remember when I mentioned to you and Maxie that I had an idea of who may have killed Joyce Abrams?"

"Of course, I do. Who could forget that?"

"Well, the note put a little doubt in my theory."

"Here we go again. More riddles. I swear, you carry on the most confusing conversations than anyone I ever met."

"How well do you know Roy Sundstrom?" Eric asked.

"Not very well. We've probably only spoken a few times. He never comes in here. Why? You think he killed Joyce?"

"No. I want to ask him a few questions, but he has no reason to talk with me. I was hoping you two knew each other, and you could introduce me."

"Sorry. I won't be any help there."

Denton looked over at the door. "Look, here comes Maxie."

Eric turned. "Oh, damn."

"What's wrong? I thought you enjoyed her company."

"I do. Or did. Let's just say, we had lunch a few days ago and things didn't go so well."

Maxie marched over to their table. "Okay if I join you?"

"Sure" Eric replied.

Denton moved over. "Sit down."

She looked at Eric. "Well, well. Let me congratulate you on turning the police department into a complete frenzy. I've been getting calls all morning about the chaos that's going on down there. You get the most influential person in the county to confess to murder. They're all scrambling trying to cover for themselves."

"I don't get it. Why are they trying to cover anything? They had no reason to link him to a crime that took place in Chicago."

She picked up a menu. "But you did."

"I had a few reasons."

"Well, my friend tells me they're all freaked out down at the station. Now they're even looking to see if Lyle could be behind Joyce's murder."

Eric shook his head. "No. That's a complete waste of time."

Denton stared at him. "There you go again. You sound like you got this one solved too."

Eric rubbed the back of his neck. "I hope not."

When their breakfasts arrived, Eric tried to get Maxie to order, but she said she'd eaten at home. They talked for another half hour, then Denton set down his napkin. "Well, another delicious breakfast." He looked over at them. "I've got a few errands to run. It was nice seeing you, Maxie."

After he left, Maxie slid closer. "I wanted to see you again. I had the feeling our lunch meeting didn't go so well. I'm sorry. I'm sure you had a lot on your mind. Did you go to the library right after our lunch?"

"No. It was later that night. "

"Well what happened?"

Eric gave her a compacted version. He left out most of the information about Cheryl.

She asked, "How long are you going to be in town this time?"

"Just a few more days. I got here almost a week ago. I don't want to wear out my welcome with Harold."

She frowned. "I'd like to see you again before you leave, but tomorrow I'm taking Dolly to Iowa for a case. You'll be gone by the time we get back."

Eric thought for a moment. "You know, you could always come and visit me in Chicago."

"Really? That would be great, but I'd have to take the train. No way would I ever attempt to drive around that city." She smiled. "I'm just a country girl, you know. I drove to Detroit once and it nearly gave me a nervous breakdown. I'm sure Chicago's a lot worse than The Motor City."

"The train would work. My apartment's not far from Union Station. Call me tomorrow and let me know how you're doing in Iowa."

"Okay." She slid closer and gave him a quick hug. "I need to get going."

As she left the diner, Eric gave a deep sigh. Was he ready for this? He reached for the check. Too late to worry about it now. He'd put out the invitation.

After paying the bill, Eric decided he needed to talk to Roy, invitation or not. The walk along the lakefront was beautiful. Roy's cabins were about a mile to the north of the diner. They were situated where the fish streets ended at the city limits.

Eric rang the bell outside the motel office. An older man with a short cigarette hanging from the corner of his mouth appeared. "If you want a cabin, I need to tell you we're closing up at the end of the month."

"I appreciate the information, but I'm not looking for a cabin. I'd like to ask you a few questions."

Roy's eye's narrowed. "Hey, wait a minute. Aren't you the guy who was on TV this morning? The guy that got Lyle Lapeer arrested?"

Eric nodded. "Yes, I —"

Roy threw the door open. "Come in. You can ask whatever the hell you want. It's about time that little weasel got arrested for something." He grimaced. "Oh, shit. I'm sorry to hear about your wife."

"Thanks." Eric stepped into the office.

Roy swept a stack of magazines over to a corner of his desk to make room. "Sit here. You want some coffee?"

"No thanks. I just came from a big breakfast over at the diner."

Roy plumped down into a worn chair behind his desk. "What's on your mind?"

"I don't know if you remember, but I was here that night they discovered the body under one of your cabins."

Roy leaned closer and squinted. "Not really. It was dark that night, and to tell you the truth, things were happening so fast most of what I remember is nothing but a blur."

"It was a very strange night."

"So what are you here for?" Roy asked.

"I was wondering if you had any records of who worked here around the time Joyce Abrams went missing."

Roy smiled. "You and a hundred cops. They asked me the same thing about a dozen times. What I told them was, that was a long time ago. Twenty years or so. I've had a lot of people working around here in all them years. Probably hundreds if you added them up. Nobody stays around long. People that work here are either young and are looking for their first job, or they're in some kinda bind and need a place to stay along with a couple of bucks. Once their problem gets taken care of they move on." He turned to a small fridge behind him and pulled out a bottle of beer. "You want one?"

"Sure." Eric needed to keep the conversation going. "I get it. But what about records. You must have kept track of how much money you were spending on employees for tax purposes."

Roy handed him a beer. "The missus took care of all that." He took a swig. "Did a damn good job too. Before she left me."

"Did she keep records of those things? Old tax filings maybe?"

"You know, come to think of it, she had a little office I set up for her in the basement. I think there's still boxes of all her crap piled up to the rafters. It's way in the back under a pile of crap. Once she was gone, I had to hire me an accountant. He never asked about them. Every year I promise myself I'll toss all that old shit out, but with all the stuff that keeps breaking on these falling down cabins, I never find the time. Maybe this winter I'll finally get to it."

"Would you mind if I take a look? I know it's a long shot, but if she's got files stored, maybe I could find some payroll records."

Roy took another swig. "You're the guy who put Lyle away. Ain't no skin off my ass if you want to get full of cobwebs down there. Come on. I'll show you where her shit's piled up."

*****

Three hours later Eric stood in front of Brian's house and knocked on the door. Nobody answered. Was he home? Maybe he'd gone to Chicago for that concert he'd mentioned a few days before.

A loud voice behind him asked, "What are you doing here?" Eric spun around.

Brian was standing behind him. He noticed Eric staring at the axe. "I was behind the shed chopping wood."

"I'm looking for you."

Brian looked at Eric's car. "Where's Harold?"

"Back at the house, I imagine."

193

"He's not with you?"

"No. I came by myself."

Brian stepped in front of the door but didn't open it. "Why are you here?"

"I wanted to ask you a few questions."

"Oh, you do, do you. What's going on? Now that you got a big head from having Lyle Lapeer arrested, you think you're some kind of private detective all of a sudden? Why the hell should I spend time answering your questions?"

Eric waited a moment. "You don't. But being a decent man, I'd think you'd be just as interested in finding out who killed that poor girl they found under Roy Sundstrom's cabin as I am. As everybody in the whole town is. But then again, maybe I'm wrong."

Brian turned, reached for the doorknob, and then stopped. "What's your question?"

"I know you were working at the cabins when Joyce disappeared. I was wondering if you could remember who else worked there at the same time."

He shook his head. "Who told you that? You got that wrong. I didn't work there then. When Joyce went missing, I was working at my folks place in Trout Creek."

"Are you sure about that?"

Brian moved the axe from one hand to the other. "Just who the hell do you think you are coming over and asking me these questions? What makes you so sure I was working at Roy's place then?"

"I saw the pay records."

Brian stepped back. "What pay records?"

"The detailed paperwork that Roy's wife kept in their basement of everyone's hours and the dates they worked."

Brian threw the axe to the ground and gave Eric a shove. "Get the hell off my property. Why the hell you're wasting your time checking up on shit I did twenty years ago is beyond me. If you think you're going to spin a bunch of tales and pin something on me just because I was dating your damn wife before you even came into the picture, you're crazy. Something's wrong with you. I'm going to give Harold a call and tell him he'd better reign you in. If you keep harassing me, you're going to find out you're not dealing with a milk toast like Lyle Lapeer. I suggest you do your snooping elsewhere." He pushed the door open and stomped into the house.

Eric stared down at the axe. That could have ended very badly.

*****

Harold was working on his manuscript in the library when Eric stepped in. He looked up from his laptop. "Where have you been? Lillian delayed lunch for an hour waiting for you. We finally decided to eat. We were starving."

"I'm sorry. I got wrapped up in something. I completely lost track of time."

"So, you didn't eat then?"

"No."

"Check out the fridge. Lillian has a chicken leg and a salad all ready for you."

"Great. I'll have to thank her."

Harold stared. "Where have you been? Looks like you've been working in a dusty coal bin somewhere."

Eric smiled. "Pretty close. I've been rummaging around Roy Sundstrom's basement."

Harold jerked back so quickly, one of his reference books fell to the floor with a thud. "Roy Sundstrom's basement? You're joking, right?"

"No. And your coal bin analogy isn't far off. The place was a mess."

"What were you doing down there?"

"Digging through twenty-year-old pay stubs which took me two hours to find."

"Pay stubs? What on earth for?"

"To find out if your friend, Brian, was working there when Joyce disappeared."

Harold removed his glasses from the top of his head and placed them on the corner of his desk. "Good Lord, Eric. I know you two don't care much for each other, but I'm getting the impression that you're working overtime to tie him to Joyce's murder somehow. Why?"

"I'm not. I thought that if he worked there then maybe he'd remember some other people who were there at the same time. Maybe somebody stood out. Somebody the police could look into."

Harold cocked his head. "Really? That's it?"

Eric paused. "Mostly. But I must tell you, I've read some disturbing things about him in Claire's diaries. Things that raised my suspicions. Nothing concrete. Nothing I'd ever discuss with anyone else. But even way back then, he didn't treat women with any respect. That made me wonder if he was working at the cabins when Joyce went missing. He told us he worked there right after high school."

"But...to take the time and energy to go over to Roy's. I hope you weren't throwing Brian's name around Roy? God knows how easy it is for rumors to start in this small town. For all I know, Brian will be featured on some crazy news story tonight about a serial killer on the loose in Red Cedar Cove."

Eric's eyebrow's shot up. "Serial killer? Is there something you're not telling me?"

Harold stood. "Damnit, Eric, that's not funny. What I'm trying to tell you is, you start asking questions around here and people are going to start making unfounded assumptions."

"Calm down, Harold. I never mentioned anyone's name. I just asked him if he knew of any pay records from way back when. He didn't think there were any but then remembered his wife used to do the books. He took me down to his basement and told me I could rummage around as much as I liked. I didn't tell him what I discovered."

"I hope not." Harold was about to say something when his cell phone rang.

Eric tried to see the name of who was calling. It had to be Brian.

Harold picked it up and listened. The longer Brian talked; the darker Harold's face got. He stood, walked to the window, mumbled a few words into the phone, and hung up.

"Why didn't you mention that you payed Brian a visit?"

"I was getting to it."

Harold returned to his desk, picked up a book, and slammed it shut. "Maybe it's time you left my friend alone."

"How about this? It seems I've hit a nerve somehow. Maybe I've overstayed your hospitality. I think it's time I give you a little space. I'm sorry I've upset you."

Harold grabbed his laptop and walked toward the door. "Maybe you're right."

After quickly gathering his belongings, Eric found himself sitting behind the wheel of his car. Had this actually happened? When he asked Harold about overstaying his hospitality, he hadn't dreamed Harold would agree. Everything escalated so quickly. Why did finding Brian's pay stubs have such an effect on Harold? What was he going to do now? Where was he going to go?

Chapter 23

JACK SHUFFLED INTO the visiting room of the county jail and sat down across from Christine. He gave her an embarrassed smile. "This is a surprise."

She didn't return his smile. "I'm here to try and find out who it was that was living next to me and my son. Was it the nice guy who both Buddy and I adored or some hardened criminal who was putting my child at risk every day I went to work?"

Jack's eyes dropped. "I guess a little of both, but I'm hoping you'll see more of the first person than the second." He looked back at her. "Both you and Buddy are owed an explanation. But you're right. I did put him at risk. I can see that now, and I'm very sorry I did that. Anyway, I'll tell you the whole damn story." He settled back in his chair and took a deep breath. "I'll start at the beginning."

She glared at him. "Please do."

"Okay. Here we go. I got out of the Army a few years ago. Did three tours in Afghanistan. When I got back, things started to go bad. I wasn't the same. My marriage fell apart. I have a fifteen-year-old daughter. It tore me up when we got divorced and I had to move out of the house. I didn't know where to go. After a few nights in a cheap motel, I went down to Grand Rapids and stayed with a friend of mine from the service. Let's just say it wasn't the smartest thing I could have done. I was living with him and going to counseling. I knew this guy was a little on the shady side, but I didn't give a damn. I needed a place to stay. Anyway, one night some guy stopped by. We finished up a couple of six-packs and my friend decided we needed to get more beer and a bottle of whiskey. We all hopped into my car

James R. Nelson

and I drove them to the liquor store. I gave them some money for a six-pack and stayed in the car. A few minutes later, they came running out. The idiots had robbed the place. They were half drunk before they got there. A customer tried to play hero and started fighting with my friend. He ended up getting shot."

Christine shook her head.

"The guy didn't die. Thank God he only got grazed on the side of his chest. Anyway, I knew I had to get out of there. I packed up my stuff in the middle of the night and came up here and rented the cabin."

She took a deep breath. "How did they find you? Why were they looking for you?"

"Probably wanted to make sure I didn't say anything. My friend had been in jail before. If he got pinched for this, he'd be looking at over twenty years. Both of them had priors. How did they find me? Johnnie was with me when we were in Kandahar. Over there you do a lot of talking. All we did on our down time was swap stories. He heard about all the times I used to come up here hunting and fishing with my father. I hated living with him in Grand Rapids. He probably thought this is where I'd end up."

She stared down at the table. "You...you put my son in jeopardy. You knew some men may come looking for you. You even told Buddy to watch out for them and to lie to them if they showed up. I'm sure you told him not to say anything about this to me too."

After a moment of silence, Jack nodded. "Yeah. I did."

She pulled a tissue from her purse and dabbed her eyes. "What's going to happen now?"

He shrugged. "I don't know."

*****

Denton looked at the two bags of groceries Eric set down on his kitchen table. "You didn't have to do that."

"I know. Don't worry, I'm only staying two days."

"Stay as long as you want. But I have to admit, I was a little surprised when I got your call. What happened anyway? I thought you and Harold were tight."

"I did too. As to what happened, let's just say after you left, I had a busy morning. Let me tell you about it."

After twenty minutes, Denton shook his head. "You're right. You hit a nerve somehow. It seems reasonable enough to ask the man if he could remember anyone else who was working there at the time, if they looked suspicious or had some kind of criminal past."

"Apparently Harold and Brian didn't see it that way. I hope Harold calms down about this. I've always considered him a good friend. I'd hate to lose that relationship now that Claire's gone."

"I'm sure you would, but maybe you're going to have to let it go. Technically he's not even your brother-in-law anymore."

"I guess, but I don't think of it that way. We've known each other for so many years. I hope this can blow over."

*****

The next morning, as Eric and Denton slid into their favorite booth at the diner, Cheryl rushed up to their table. She had a big smile. "Guess what, guys?"

Denton was the first to respond. "Is it free coffee day?"

She waved her hand. "Very funny. No. I'm pretty sure I know who my father is."

"Who?" Eric asked.

"Remember that guy Lyle kept accusing me of working with?"

"His nephew?"

"Yes. His name's Paul Sykes, and he really is Lyle's nephew."

"Who's Paul Sykes?" Denton asked.

Cheryl turned. "Aren't you listening? He's Lyle's nephew, and he says he's my father."

"Are you sure?" Eric asked. "How do you know this?"

"I had a long talk with him and Roy yesterday. Paul told me all about how he and my mother were in love, and that when my mother got pregnant, he went to ask his uncle for help. It's a long, sad story. But he's very happy to know me, and so is Roy." She looked over at the cash register. "Oh, there's Mrs. Smithfield. I need to go." She paused. "I forgot to take your order. Is it going to be the usual?"

Denton nodded.

Eric said, "Yes."

"I'll be right back with your coffees."

As Cheryl left, Eric asked, "Do you know this guy?"

Denton shook his head. "Never heard of him, but he must have spent some time around here if he was able to get Roy's daughter pregnant." He drummed his fingers on the table. "I hope this doesn't turn out to be bad news for Cheryl. Roy's a pretty rough character."

"You're right about that. When I was listening to Lyle talk to Cheryl, he sure didn't have a very good opinion about his nephew."

Denton frowned. "Ah, I don't think Lyle's opinion means very much around here anymore, if you know what I mean."

"No kidding." The buzz of a cell phone cut him short. He pulled it out of his pocket. "It's Harold. I wonder if I should take it?"

"Go ahead. He's probably thought about what he's said, and how he's treated you, and now he wants to make amends."

Eric put the phone up to his ear. "Hello." He listened as Harold talked. Eric asked, "Are you sure? Today? Well, I guess. Okay. I'll see you there." He hung up and looked over at Denton. "That was odd."

"What?"

"He apologized a few times and said he thought it would be a good idea if we met up at Ledge Park and did some of the trails like we talked about. He said it would be a good time to clear the air and patch things up."

"Ledge Park? Harold wants to go hiking?"

"I know. It sounds crazy, but it's something we mentioned several times."

Denton looked at him from the corner of his eye. "When you going?"

"I'm supposed to meet him at three o'clock."

Chapter 24

AT FIVE MINUTES to three, Eric stepped out of his car and looked around. The parking lot was empty. A cool breeze was blowing off the lake. It was a perfect day for hiking.

A few minutes later Harold's car turned into the parking lot and pulled up next to him. Harold jumped out, ran up, and extended his hand. "Damn, Eric. I'm so sorry we had words yesterday. I...I'm ashamed of myself. I told Lillian what happened, and she gave me a good talking to. I hope you'll accept my apology."

"Of course, I do. And maybe I've been focusing a little too much on your friend—"

"No. Let's not talk about him. Let's just relax, enjoy this beautiful day, and take that hike we've been promising ourselves for about a month now." He looked over and saw a large map mounted at the trail head. "Let's head over there and see where these trails go. Didn't Brian...ah, I've heard that the Ledge trail is great. It's got spectacular views over the lake and it's not as hilly as the other two. I say we try that one."

When they got to the map, three trails were marked, each one with a different color. Eric grabbed a brochure with a much smaller version of the same map.

"Think we're going to get lost?" Harold asked.

"It's not what I'm planning on, but since neither of us has hiked here before, it's always a good idea to have a map." Eric pointed to a small sign with a blue arrow. He glanced back at the big map "That sign shows us where the trail starts. Blue is for the Ledge trail. The other ones have red and yellow colors."

Harold stepped toward where the sign indicated. "Guess all we have to do is follow the blue markings."

Fifty feet ahead was a large pine tree with a daub of blue about eight feet up the trunk. Eric pointed. "Looks like this is where we start."

They stepped under a thick canopy of pine branches. Twenty feet into the trail, the temperature dropped a few degrees and long shadows replaced the sunny open spaces of the parking lot. Contrary to what Harold said, the trail climbed steadily upward. After twenty minutes, Harold said, "I don't know about you, but I need to stop for a while. My legs are killing me."

Eric motioned to a fallen log. "Mine too." He sat down. "I just didn't want to be the first one to stop."

Harold sat down next to him. "I knew I was out of shape, but this is ridiculous. When I was a kid, I could have hiked this trail four times in a row. Damn Lillian's killing me with those homemade desserts of hers."

A branch cracked about twenty feet behind them. Eric turned and stared into the woods. "I'd think there'd be some deer on this trail."

"I thought we might see a few in the field next to the parking area. Probably have a better chance to see a mountain goat on this damn trail."

Eric smiled. "Now don't get carried away, Harold. We're not in Colorado." He stood. "Shall we continue?"

"I guess. It sure seems like it's the Rocky's." Harold slowly stood and rubbed the front of his legs. "We've got to be almost up to that ledge by now."

After another ten minutes, Eric saw a sign that pointed to the right. *Ledge Trail Overlook.* The trail evened out and the view was amazing. As he stood looking out over the lake hundreds of feet below, Harold caught up with him.

Harold took a few short breaths and leaned against a tree. "I guess it was worth it."

As Eric stepped out onto several huge boulders to get a better look, there was a rustling in the bushes behind Harold. Brian stepped out of the woods. He had a gun strapped to his side.

"What are you doing here?" Harold asked. "I thought you were in Chicago?"

"I was about to leave when you called. When I heard you guys were going hiking, I thought it was an opportunity I didn't want to miss."

As Eric attempted to move away from the steep drop-off, Brian pulled out his gun. "Stay right where you are. You're good there."

Harold spun around. "What the hell's going on? Brian, put that damn gun back."

Brian took a few steps closer and continued to train the gun on Eric. "I don't think so. Our little amateur detective's been sticking his nose where it doesn't belong. I guess his head got big when he figured out Lyle killed his wife. Now he wants to pin Joyce's murder on me. Now Harold, you wouldn't want that to happen, would you?" Brian shot a quick glance toward Harold. "Maybe you need to tell him something."

"He was just trying to find out who worked at Roy's place when you did, Brian. That doesn't mean anything. Plenty of kids worked there. I think you're overreacting. There's nothing that proves—"

"That you killed her, Harold?" Eric asked.

Harold stopped breathing for a few moments. He swallowed hard. "What are you talking about? Are you crazy?"

"Everything in Claire's diaries pointed to Brian until Lillian told me about the code Claire was using. The letter B didn't refer to Brian like I thought for so long, did it. It was an abbreviation for brother. Once I learned that, things suddenly changed. When you were home from college for the summer, you fell pretty hard for Joyce, didn't you? What happened? How did she die?"

Harold was sweating. "Don't say anything, Brian. It's just a trap. He doesn't know."

"I know as much as your sister did. She wrote some nasty things about you after Joyce went missing. Seems like Claire was there that night. Along with you, Brian, and Joyce. It's interesting the police never found out about that. You all did a pretty good job of keeping your mouths shut."

Brian pulled the gun's hammer back with his thumb. "Don't worry about a trap. Eric's going to take a nasty fall. He won't be telling anybody about what we did."

Harold took a step toward Brian. "No. We can reason with him."

"Reason my ass. He hasn't been snooping around here so he can reason with us. I knew it wasn't good when you told me Lillian gave him those damn diaries. I broke into the house and tried to steal them. None of this shit would have ever happened if I could have laid my hands on them."

"What?" Harold exclaimed. "You pushed Lillian down the stairs?"

"She got in the way. I had to get out of there when she came poking around."

Eric turned back to Harold. "Why did Claire think you killed Joyce, Harold?"

"Because we were arguing in the bedroom of Brian's cabin. We were both pretty drunk. I don't really know what happened. We both passed out. When I woke up, Joyce wasn't breathing. She had thrown up all over the bathroom. She was lying next to the toilet."

"Why do you think you killed her?" Eric asked.

"I...I didn't help her. I should have been there when she was choking."

Brian stepped closer and aimed the gun at Eric's head. "Enough talking. It's time for you to take a fall. Step over closer to the cliff."

Eric glanced towards the woods. Was there someplace he could run? The closest trees were twenty feet away on either side of him. Two steps and Brian would shoot him. He had to stall for time. "Who buried her under the cabin? Don't tell me. I bet that was Brian's idea." He looked over at Harold. "No wonder you kept up your friendship with him so long. He had a secret that you didn't want to come out."

Brian stepped closer. "Secrets? Yeah, we got a lot of them. Here's one for you, Harold. Joyce wasn't dead when I dumped her in that hole under the cabin. I had her half covered up when she started moaning. Scared the hell out of me. I had to grab a cement block and put her out of her misery."

Harold fell to the ground. "No...no. All this time you made me think it was my fault." He glared at Brian. "So, all these years you've been holding this over my head and...and...it was you that killed her?"

"Served her right. That little tease thought she could drink all our liquor, parade around in her underwear, and then get all huffy when we wanted to have a little fun."

Harold looked up. There were tears in his eyes. "She was alive? Why...why did you have to kill her?"

"How the hell was I going to explain she was in a hole in the ground, and I was the guy shoveling dirt over her? You got an answer for that? Jeez, Harold, it doesn't matter. It's still only you and me who knows what—"

A gunshot echoed through the woods and a piece of granite next to Brian's foot exploded against his leg. He let out a yell, bent down, and felt blood.

Denton stepped out of the woods holding a deer rifle. "Let go of the gun or I'll drop you like a dead moose."

As Brian swung the revolver toward him, Denton fired. A bullet zipped past Brian's ear. Eric grabbed his arm. He struggled with Brian for the gun. Denton ran over and smashed the butt of the rifle against Brian's head. Eric twisted the gun from his grip. With blood pouring from his temple, Brian got hold of Denton and pulled him to the ground.

Eric pointed the revolver at the two men wrestling among the boulders. "Get off him, Brian. I swear, I'll shoot you."

They clawed at each other as they rolled closer to the edge. Eric tried to aim, but they were moving so fast, he was afraid he'd hit Denton if he fired.

Harold yelled, "Watch out. The cliff!"

Eric reached for Denton.

Like a slow-motion movie, Brian and Denton disappeared over the precipice.

Chapter 25

ERIC RUSHED OVER to the ledge. Two bodies lay crumpled on a narrow outcrop of rock about twenty feet below. He yelled, "Denton! Are you okay?" There was no response. Eric called out again.

A weak voice floated up from below, "My back. I can't move!"

Harold slowly stepped near the edge and peered over. "Brian?"

"I...I think he's dead." Denton moaned. "I landed on top of him." Denton slowly raised his head. "I'm in a lot of pain. I need help."

Eric looked for a way to climb down. The drop off was sheer. There was nothing to hold or grab on to. "I'm calling now. Just lie still. Don't move."

As they waited for help to arrive, Harold said, "It's over for me."

"What do you mean?"

"You heard what happened. I'm going to jail."

Eric looked at him. "But you didn't kill her. Brian did."

Harold took a step closer to the cliff. "What difference does it make? I thought I did. I didn't know what to do. He...he said I shouldn't say anything. He'd hide the body for me. I panicked. I didn't try and get help. I'm going down. Murder, attempted murder, manslaughter, what the hell's the difference."

Harold slowly inched closer to the edge. "When this comes out, my reputation's over. All my research, gone. Done. The book I'm working on is meaningless. Three years down the drain. I'll be a laughingstock. Who's going to take my work seriously when this comes out?"

He spun around and lunged toward the drop-off. He teetered on the edge. "I can't live like that. Locked up like an animal."

"Harold. Stop! You don't know what's going to happen I heard Brian say he killed her. You need to—"

Harold looked over the edge. "It'll be quick. Then everything will be over. I won't have to—"

"Please. Think of Lillian."

"Tell her I'm so...."

Eric dove for his brother-in-law. He grabbed him by his shirt sleeve and pulled him back. "This isn't the answer. It's a coward's way out." He shoved him to the ground. "You're just going to have to deal with it."

*****

"What are all the boxes for?" Buddy asked.

"We've got to be out of here in two weeks. We need to get ready to move. I've been stopping at the market and picking up boxes whenever I can. It's not easy finding something big enough to use."

"Where we going?"

His mother let out a long sigh. "I don't know. Everything I look at is out of my budget." There was a loud knock at the door. She glanced up at the clock. Who'd be visiting at eight-thirty at night?

Buddy moved toward the door.

"No, Buddy. I'll get it."

She walked to the living room and peered out the window. A man she didn't know was standing on the porch. She pulled back. Who was he? Was he someone from Jack's problem?

Buddy came up behind her. "Who is it?"

"I don't know. I'm not opening the door."

James R. Nelson

Buddy crawled up on the couch and peeked out the window. "It's Paul."

"You know this guy?"

"Yeah. He's the one who saved us. The man from the island."

Christine pressed her face closer to the window. "Buddy, he doesn't look anything like that guy."

"It's him, Mom. He got his hair cut. Let him in."

"What's he want with us at this time of night?"

"How you gonna know if you don't open the door?"

She pulled the door open a few inches. "Can I help you?"

"Yes. Jack sent me. I'm sorry it's so late, but I've been working on a house over at Trout Creek. I thought I'd stop by on the way home. It won't take long." He looked behind her. "Hi, Buddy. How are you?"

"Good." He turned back to his mother and whispered. "Let him in, Ma."

She slowly pushed the door open. "Come in."

"Thank you." He stepped into the living room. "I promise I won't be long. I stopped in to see Jack today and he wanted to let you know that he's rented the house I'm working on."

"He did? Why are you telling me that and …isn't he being a bit hasty? I mean, he could be looking at a lot of time in jail. At least, that's what he told me when I visited him. Are they letting him go?"

"Oh, no…no. I'm sorry. He rented it for you and Buddy."

Christine stepped back. "What?"

"Yes. He's paid for the first six months. I know you guys need to be out of here at the end of the month. That's why I've been working so late every night. I'm pretty sure I'll have everything ready by next Monday so you could start moving your things over there then."

212

A rush of excitement went through her. "That's great news because I've been looking, but it's been impossible to find anything." She stopped. "But…I can't accept that. With his problem, won't he need money for an attorney?"

Paul shrugged. "I asked him the same thing. This is what he wants to do."

"I don't know. I'm not sure I can do this. I'm going to have to talk to him. It…it just doesn't seem right."

Paul turned and stepped toward the door. "The house is at 247 Grove Street. I'll be working there the next few days. Let me know what you want to do. It's a nice place. I think you'll like it."

"Wait a minute!"

As he turned back, Christine took his hand between hers. "Thank you for what you did on the island."

Paul smiled. "No thanks needed. I'm glad I was able to help."

Chapter 26

(Six Months Later)

CHERYL STEPPED INTO cabin number seven and looked around. "Roy's not going to believe it when he gets back from Arizona. I can't wait to start planting flowers."

Paul wiped sweat from his forehead. "They look pretty nice, don't they?"

"Still nicely rustic, but up to date at the same time."

"I'm hoping to get number eight done before he gets back, but I'm not sure that's going to happen."

Cheryl started to laugh.

"What's so funny?"

"I was just thinking, you modernizing these cabins is just like what I did with Roy."

Paul put down his hammer. "You lost me."

"You're spiffing up the cabins to make them look nice. Remember how I made Roy throw away those damn coveralls of his?"

Paul smiled. "Okay. I get it I couldn't believe what he looked like when he stepped out of the bedroom wearing some of the new clothes you picked out for him." Paul ran his fingers through his hair. "Roy looked better than I did when you made him shave and get his hair cut."

"Do you think he's still stopped drinking?" Cheryl asked.

Paul thought for a moment. "I hope so. After the hell you gave him, I don't think he'd want to show up here with a beer in his hand."

"When you're ready to take a break, come into the office. I want to show you some of the new marketing materials I put together."

"More materials? We're already booked for the first two weeks."

She smiled. "I know. We've got to maximize the opportunity Roy's given us."

*****

Eric helped Lillian load the last few boxes into her sister's white van. He shut the back door and said, "I'll miss you."

"It's not that far to Green Bay. I hope you'll come and visit me now and then."

"I will. I promise."

She stepped closer. "Take good care of Maxie. She's a wonderful woman. It makes me so happy when I see you together. I know you don't want to rush into anything. After what you've been through, I understand. But you two have chemistry I never saw…um, before."

Eric smiled. "I know. I'm very happy to have your endorsement. It means a lot to me."

She turned and stared at the house. "Thirty-six years. Can you believe it?" She shook her head. "Harold was a brilliant man, but he was cold like his father. Three wives. They all seemed to be nice women. I don't think he could stay married because of what haunted him. What he had done with that girl."

"Lillian, before you go, I always wanted to ask you. You insisted that I read those diaries. Did you look through them?"

She looked down. "A little. How could I not? I found them three months after Claire died. I couldn't help myself. I picked one up only because I wanted to remember Claire as a pretty little girl. I was confused by the letters and initials at first too. But I remember her calling Harold 'B'. I didn't like the things I was reading. Especially when Harold and Brian were together. I certainly never connected anything I read to poor Joyce's disappearance. But when you came by, and I heard some of the things you were asking Harold about Brian, I started having doubts."

"When you left me that note about the B meaning Brother, not Brian, I was sick about it. I had been so sure that Brian had something to do with Joyce. It was a shock when I had to reevaluate everything and start looking at Harold. I'll tell you; it was hard coming down those stairs the last few days and trying to pretend everything was just fine."

"When do you think he'll get out?"

"With both Denton and me repeating what we heard, it being an accident on Harold's part, and what Brian did, I'm hoping in a few years. It's wrong what he did, very wrong. He needs to pay a price."

She looked back at the house. "I'm looking forward to a change. My sister's health is declining. I'm glad I can be there for her." She climbed behind the wheel of the van. "Thank you again for all your help and don't forget, you promised you'd come and visit."

Eric stood in the driveway and waved as she pulled onto Lakeshore Drive. Harold had wanted him to take over the house. At least stay there when he was visiting. Not a good idea. There were too many memories of Claire. Maxie deserved better. His place in Chicago was up for sale. How long would it take before it sold?

The small house he had bought outside of Trout Creek was on a beautiful inland lake. He had driven back and forth from Chicago almost every two weeks. Maxie was getting to be more familiar with Chicago, but she insisted they keep separate places. At least for a while. There was one last thing he had wanted to do in the Windy City before his place sold and it was going to happen the next day.

*****

Denton stood in Eric's living room and stared out at Lake Michigan from the twenty-third floor. "Wow. Are you sure you want to sell this?"

"I am. I need a fresh start. The city was fun when I was younger, but now I enjoy the peace and quiet of Trout Creek."

"Well, I'm glad you invited me for the week-end." He looked over at Maxie. "What do you think? Will you miss coming here?"

"A little. But I don't think I'd ever get used to all the traffic and the noise."

Denton noticed a copy of *Death in a Small Town* sitting on a coffee table. He picked it up. "I still can't believe it was you who wrote this. I can't imagine what it felt like for you to watch as your wife was getting all those accolades and then the MacIntosh Award."

Eric smiled. "I have to admit, at times it wasn't easy. There was a time when Harold took me over to Brian's house and Brian was really giving me hell about how successful Claire was as a writer. He wasn't really complimenting Claire. He was putting me down. I had all I could do that day to keep my mouth shut."

Denton shook his head. "It's quite a book. At least now, the truth is out."

"You know what's funny about that book?" Eric asked.

Both Maxie and Denton asked, "What?"

"It drove guilty people crazy."

217

"What do you mean?" Maxie asked.

"Because Harold and Lyle thought Claire wrote it, they kept thinking some of the characters were about real people from Red Cedar Cove. Lyle was upset with Claire because he thought she had put things in about his nephew. Harold and Brian were worried she had put subtle little things in the book about Joyce. They didn't know I wrote it and had no idea that Lyle Lapeer even had a nephew. Claire had mentioned a few times that one of her friends had disappeared, but it wasn't something she ever dwelled on."

Denton nodded. "You're right. Hidden guilt created things in their heads that weren't there."

There was a knock. Maxie looked over at Eric and smiled.

As Eric walked to the door, he looked back at Denton. "Remember I told you there was someone I wanted you to meet?"

"Yes. You were very vague about who it was."

Eric opened the door. "Charles. Come in. You know Maxie. I'd like you to meet my friend, Denton Morris."

Charles stuck out his hand. "Charles Hebbard. Nice to meet you."

"Nice to meet you too."

As everyone took a seat, Eric said, "Denton, Charles is my agent."

Denton nodded. "I see."

Charles asked, "How are you doing? Eric's told me about what happened to you."

"I'm good as new. I bruised my spine when I went over that cliff. I spent a few days in the hospital. Then three months of physical therapy got me back on my feet. I feel fine now. Thank you for asking."

"Eric's also told me quite a bit about your writing and what you've done in the past. He's given me some of the work you've done in that critique group you belong to."

Denton's eyes widened. "No. Eric. That was just me messing around. You shouldn't have. It was never meant to be read by...by an agent."

Eric smiled. "Calm down, Denton. It was good. No, it was great."

"I agree," Charles said. "I'm here hoping you'll let me work with you. I think it's time for you to get the recognition you deserve. I've got a few ideas for new projects that I'd like to present to some of the publishers I work with. What do you say?"

Denton turned to Eric. "You set me up, didn't you? You got me to come to Chicago under a false pretense."

Eric smiled. "I did. I was tired of watching you laze around all day when I had to be busy working on my latest book. I thought it was time for you to suffer the same fate. What do you say?"

Denton turned to Charles. "I say...bring it on."

*****

Buddy jumped out of Jack's boat and made sure the anchor was set in the soft, white sand that surrounded Winter Island.

Jack put his arm around Christine. "It's good to breathe fresh air again."

She snuggled into his shoulder. "I can only imagine."

"If Johnny hadn't testified that he held a gun on me and made me drive away that night, I'd never be standing here right now."

She shook her head. "And if Johnny hadn't been stupid enough to rob that place, you wouldn't have had to put up with everything."

Jack kissed her cheek. "But then I wouldn't have met you, would I?"

She laughed and pushed him away. "I think you're giving Johnny too much credit. Don't forget about the eight guys who were in your squad in Afghanistan who showed up and testified for you."

He nodded. "Yeah. That was a surprise."

She turned to him. "How come you never told me you won a Purple Heart over there?"

"Why would I? I have enough nightmares about that place."

A tall girl jumped out of the boat. "Where's this tree house you keep telling me about, Buddy?"

"Come on. I'll show you."

Jack's daughter ran after him through the woods.

Christine took Jack's hand. "They seem to be getting along okay."

"Are you kidding? She loves Buddy. She always complained about being an only child."

They walked along the path and stopped at the base of the tree house.

"Come on up," Buddy called.

Jack craned his neck "In a minute." He looked around the forest.

Christine asked, "What's the matter? Is something on your mind?"

"I was just thinking about Winter Island."

"What about it?"

"Look what's happened because two kids decided to sneak over here and build a tree house."

Christine looked puzzled. "What?"

"Buddy and his dog found a human bone. Two girls, who were missing for twenty years were finally accounted for. I met Paul and we've got a nice little house to live in. I've put my past troubles behind me. We're both working good jobs. And my daughters finally got the brother she's always wanted."

Christine smiled. "You're right. All because of Winter Island."

THE END

(If you enjoyed this book, the author would appreciate a review on Amazon.com, Goodreads, Facebook, etc. Thank you.)

Other Books by James R. Nelson

The Stephen Moorehouse Mystery Series

The Butterfly Conspiracy
The Peacock Prophecy
Menagerie of Broken Dreams
The Monarch Graveyard

The Archie Archibald Mystery Series

A Crimson Sky for Dying
The Black Orchid Mystery
Unsafe Harbor

Stand Alone Titles

The Pilot
The Maze at Four Chimneys
The House on Turner Lane
Peacock Redux and Other Short Stories

Contact Information

Email – jrnfl@hotmail.com
Website – jamesrnelson.com

**A Preview of another novel by
James R. Nelson.**

The House on Turner Lane

Prologue

FOREST RANGER CHARLIE Loonsfoot slammed on the brakes as he rounded a steep corner on South Boundary Road. Two black bear cubs scrambled out of his way and played next to an outcrop of rock. By the size of them, they were probably around seven months old and both males. They were born in January when their mother was still in hibernation.

Charlie watched as they wrestled with each other. He peered out of his rain-spotted windshield. Where was she? Close. Mama wouldn't be far from her cubs. They'd better enjoy their time with her now because next summer she'd be snapping at them to go off on their own.

He hit the gas pedal and continued up the steep road. It was nice to get out of that damn office. He was proud of his promotion, but now it kept him behind a desk most of the time. He pulled into an overlook area and turned up the heater, but he knew it was no use. The government truck he grabbed from the motor pool had problems. He rubbed his hands together and flipped on the two-way radio. Nothing urgent. Just typical chatter. Not much was going on. The cold front and rain squalls that rolled in a few days before were enough to nearly empty the park. It sure didn't feel like July.

The two cubs he'd seen, and probably about two thousand other bears that roamed the 60,000-acre Porcupine Mountain Wilderness State Park, had the place almost to themselves.

He rubbed condensation off his window and looked outside. There was nothing to see. A gray mist hung over the mountains.

Back down the road, one of the bear cubs stopped and sniffed the air. He walked closer to a flat spot fifty feet off the pavement where the ground had been disturbed. He pawed at the dirt a few times and then dug deeper. Curious, his sibling wandered over and joined in. The glint of a thin gold necklace was ignored as the rancid smell of decay captured their attention.

Slowly they uncovered a human skull and pried it from the ground. The first cub batted it and chased after it as it rolled down an incline. His brother ran over, bit down between the eye sockets, and tried to yank the skull away.

From a dense thicket their mother gave a sharp bark. The two cubs released their newly found toy and scampered toward her. The dropped skull rolled down a small hill and splashed into a fast-moving creek where it bobbed along the surface for a few minutes before sinking. The strong current carried it downstream tumbling unseen from the surface, among the stones and gravel of the creek bed.

Chapter 1

OLIVIA THOMPSON BRUSHED away tears as she slipped out of her mother's bedroom and quietly closed the door behind her. She sat down at the kitchen table. "I hope it's my imagination, Elaine, but I think Mom looks even thinner now than she did when I got home from college." She picked up a napkin and dabbed her eyes.

"I don't think so. They've been monitoring her weight every time I take her to the clinic. It may have gone down a little, but Doctor Franz thinks things have actually started to stabilize."

Olivia reached over and took Elaine's hand. "What would we do without you?"

"Just stop now. Your mother and I have been best friends ever since your family moved here." She smiled. "You girls were so adorable. Just think, you were only three and your sister was almost six." She stared at Olivia. "Look at you now. A whole year of college behind you."

Olivia glanced at the clock above the stove. "Speaking of Rachel, why isn't she here?"

Elaine sighed. "I think she's having a hard time facing the fact that your mother's sick. She...she seems to think this is going to go away somehow."

Olivia went over to the coffeepot. "You want a refill?"

"Sure." Elaine handed her a cup.

Olivia poured them both coffee and sat back down. "You're making excuses for her just like Mom always does. She has a hard time facing anything. Getting a job, keeping a job, getting a boyfriend, keeping a boyfriend..." She took a sip. "I'm sorry. I shouldn't vent. But while I was gone, she should've been over here doing all the things you've been doing. Sometimes I...I just don't understand her."

"I'm over here doing things I want to be doing. If it was me, you know your mother would be at my place doing the same things I'm doing for her." She picked up her cup. "Remember when your dad got sick? Rachel didn't handle that very well either. She was shocked when your father finally passed. Everyone else saw it coming."

Olivia dabbed her eyes again. "You're being too kind. Rachel was always too busy with her own issues to worry about Dad. She's self-centered. That's all there is to it." She brushed a lock of hair away from her face. Maybe that's why they were never close.

She picked up her cellphone and punched in a number. "Rachel, it's three-thirty. You were supposed to be here at three. Are you on your way?" Her face tightened. "Maybe tomorrow? That's your answer?" After another minute, she ended the call and set the phone back down.

During the conversation, Elaine had left the table and was busying herself straightening up the kitchen.

"I hate to ask," Olivia said, "but can you stay another hour?"

"Sure. I need to be home at five when Ben gets there, but dinners already in the Crock Pot."

Olivia grabbed her purse. "I need to have a little talk with my sister. You know, face to face."

As she drove down North Street, Olivia was surprised to see how many more businesses were closed since the last time she'd visited her sister. Once the docks shut down and the huge ore boats stopped coming, the many bars that lined the street just couldn't make it. Was Beamer's Tavern still open? Just like Rachel to live above a bar.

When Olivia rounded the corner, she had her answer. Several cars were in the parking lot, and music blasted from inside. She climbed halfway up the old wooden steps to her sister's apartment and then stopped in panic. The handrail she was holding onto swayed back and forth. It felt like the whole staircase could collapse at any minute. How could Rachel live here?

Olivia caught her breath and carefully climbed the rest of the way to her sister's door. She knocked. There was no answer. She knocked again, then peeked into a side window. Dirty dishes were stacked on the kitchen counter. Was Rachel out somewhere?

Olivia turned and cautiously made her way back down the rickety staircase. She passed the door to the tavern and stopped. Could Rachel be inside? She pressed her face close to the big plate glass window. Yes, there she was having a drink at the bar. Olivia entered the building and took a seat next to her.

Rachel turned to her in surprise. "What are you doing here? Out slummin'?" She motioned to the bartender. "Hey, Gene, get my sister a drink. Put it on my tab."

Olivia reached into her purse and tossed some money on the bar. "I'll pay for my own drink, thank you."

"What are you having?" the bartender asked.

"Cabernet Sauvignon, please.'"

Rachel's eyebrows arched. "Did you hear that? Cabernet Sauvignon." She looked down the length of the bar. "We're all drinking Bud Lite, but the queen here wants Cabernet Sauvignon."

Ignoring her sister's comment, Olivia replied, "It's nice to see you too. I've been home three weeks now, and I've only seen you a few times."

"I've been…busy." Rachel pulled a cigarette from a pack on the bar and lit it.

Olivia waved the smoke away. "Mom was looking forward to seeing you today."

"Really? The last time I was over there all she did was sleep. When she finally did wake up, all she did was talk about how happy she was that you were home."

"Elaine from next door is helping out a lot. I thought that, since you're not working, and I'm home now, we could both figure out a schedule and let Elaine get back to doing her own things."

Rachel grimaced. "A schedule? Don't sign me up for any schedule. I've been looking for a job. It's not easy finding something around here. When an opening does come up, I've gotta jump on it. I can't be tied down to any schedule."

Olivia stood. "That's what I thought you'd say." She turned toward the door.

Rachel looked at Olivia's glass. It was still three-fourth's full. "What about your drink?"

Olivia didn't respond. She continued walking toward the entrance.

"Suit yourself." Rachel picked up the glass and chugged the wine.

Chapter 2

OLIVIA CARRIED THE lunch tray into her mother's room and gently set it down on the table next to the bed. "You're looking better, Mom. You have more color than you did the last few days. Are you ready for some lunch?"

Joyce Thompson slowly pushed herself up to a sitting position. "I do feel better. And for the first time in weeks, I'm actually hungry." She looked over at the tray. "Let me start with the apple slices. They look good."

Olivia smiled and handed her the small plate of fruit. "Here. I'm so happy I don't have to argue and try to convince you to eat something."

Joyce took a bite. "The doctor said I should be starting to feel better soon. I didn't think it would take so long." Her mother slowly ate more of her lunch.

Olivia sat back in amazement. She was eating better than she had since Olivia returned from college. She couldn't wait to tell Elaine.

Her mother patted her lips with a napkin. "I heard you talking to your boyfriend this morning. He's been calling you a lot lately. I think this is more serious than you've let on."

Olivia shook her head. "No, I guess he just misses me, that's all."

"You haven't told me much about him. What's his name?"

"That's because we haven't gone out that many times. I only met him about a month before school got out. His name's Thomas. Thomas Riggins."

"Based on all the times he calls you; I think you must have made quite an impression on the young man."

8

"Please, Mother." She needed to change the subject. "He's not a young man. He was a Marine, and he's going to school on the GI Bill."

Joyce looked up. "How old is he?"

Olivia thought. "I'd say he's in his late twenties."

"How did you meet him?"

"He knew one of my girlfriends. They went to high school together. I met him down in the student union, and we kind of hit it off."

"Does he want to come by and see you? If he does, why don't you have him over?"

"He's going up to the mountains to do some hiking, and he wants me to go with him."

Joyce turned. "You should go."

Olivia sat back. "But I want to be here with you."

Joyce reached over and patted her daughter's hand. "Thank you. I know you do. But you have a life too. You've hardly left my side since you got back. I think getting out of this house would do you good."

Olivia handed her mother a small glass of milk. "No, this is where I want to be."

"I really think you should go. When does he want to go hiking?"

"It doesn't matter, Mom. I'm not going anywhere."

One hundred and sixty miles to the north, Russo's Tavern occupied a corner of the third block of the small main street of Ontonagon, Michigan for seventy-three years. With a steadily declining population—currently at 1,308—, the bar depended on visitors to the huge Porcupine Mountain Wilderness State Park to stay open.

The front door opened. Bartender Paul Karppenin turned to see who had come in. He smiled. "Hey, Charlie. I was just thinking about you."

Charlie sat down at the long bar. "Oh?"

"Well, I guess I was really thinking about me first and then you. I was wondering if you heard anything about my application."

Charlie shook his head as Paul set a tall mug of beer in front of him. "No, we've got a hiring freeze going on from Washington. Not sure how long that's going to be in effect."

Paul frowned. "Damn. I need to find a job. It would be great if I could work for the park. I'd be outside most of the time. It would be nice to get back into the woods."

"How's your degree coming?"

"Ah, kind of slow. I'm taking a few classes online, but I don't think I'll have my bachelor's degree for another year and a half."

Charlie took a sip of beer. "That may be a problem." He smiled. "You want to get back to the woods. Once I got my master's, they stuck me behind a desk. I get to drive around every now and then, but most of the time I'm pushing a pencil. Are they still closing this place?"

"As far as I know. Tearing the whole building down and putting up a car wash."

Charlie shook his head. "A car wash. I can't believe it. How'd they ever push that through the planning commission?"

Paul smiled. "When Fred Mattson speaks, everyone listens."

"Yep. Money and power. They go hand in hand. It's a shame this old building's going to have to go." He looked around the bar. "It's got so much character."

"To say nothing about putting us all out of work. Anyway, enough of that. When are they going to reopen the Summit Peak Trail?"

"It reopened last week. We didn't want to make a big deal of it, so we kept it kind of low-keyed."

"That poor hiker. I bet he doesn't get lost from now on."

"Yeah. He spent a long night up on the Summit Peak Trail." Charlie leaned forward and lowered his voice. "That's what I came in here to tell you, but you can't mention it to anybody. It hasn't made the news yet."

Paul stepped closer. Why had Charlie lowered his voice? There were only three other customers in the bar. Two of them were sitting at a table near the entrance. The other guy, Duck Lindquist, was sitting by himself at the far end of the bar. Paul asked, "What's going on?"

"Did I tell you that at first when they found the guy, they thought he was all upset about having to spend all night in the woods? But when they finally got him calmed down, that wasn't it at all. He led them to a spot off the trail where he'd found that skull."

"No. I never heard all the particulars."

"Well, tomorrow we're having a meeting up at headquarters. We're getting a briefing from the coroner and forensic anthropologist."

"How long has it been since they found the skull?"

Charlie thought. "Five or six weeks, I think."

Paul grabbed a glass and poured himself a soda. "I wonder what they figured out. That should be interesting."

Available on Amazon.com as an eBook, Paperback, and an Audible file you can listen to.

Made in the USA
Columbia, SC
12 October 2020